Pogey, Poutine and Warm, Furry Beavers

Pogey, Poutine and Warm, Furry Beavers

(Plus Twenty Other Reasons to Enjoy Being Canadian)

DAVID TOWNSEND

iUniverse, Inc.
New York   Bloomington

Pogey, Poutine and Warm, Furry Beavers
(Plus Twenty Other Reasons to Enjoy Being Canadian)

This is a work of fiction. All of the characters, names, incidents, organizations, and dialogue in this novel are either the products of the author's imagination or are used fictitiously.

iUniverse books may be ordered through booksellers or by contacting:

iUniverse
1663 Liberty Drive
Bloomington, IN 47403
www.iuniverse.com
1-800-Authors (1-800-288-4677)

Because of the dynamic nature of the Internet, any Web addresses or links contained in this book may have changed since publication and may no longer be valid. The views expressed in this work are solely those of the author and do not necessarily reflect the views of the publisher, and the publisher hereby disclaims any responsibility for them.

ISBN: 978-1-4401-9099-5 (pbk)
ISBN: 978-1-4401-9100-8 (ebk)

Printed in the United States of America

iUniverse rev. date: 12/3/2009

Contents

Introduction

So I was sprawled slug-like on the sofa the other evening, as is my custom, absently brushing the Tortilla chip crumbs out of my mustache and half-listening to *The National*, when the CBC finally got me to snap.

The approach was surprisingly simple, and effective—as it turned out, all Pastor Mansbridge had to do was cut to one of those "person-on-the-street" interviews, in which several "ordinary Canadians" were invited to yammer on a bit about the latest Weighty-News-Issue-Du-Jour.

Now, I'm not going to let on yet just what these people were saying that actually pushed me over the edge. Could be it was a coupla effete, latte-slurping, sensitive-weenie types, burbling their typical knee-jerk pieties about this country's systemic, long-standing and entirely irredeemable racism/sexism/classism/lookism, etc.

Or it might have been some of them there mouth-breathing, crimson-necked troglodytes, denouncing "immig'ants" and "Kweebecers"—you know, the kind of backwards-ass, cousin-diddling, "it blowed up real good," hairy-knuckle draggers that make the hillbillies in *Deliverance* look like assistant professors from U of T.

Doesn't really matter much either way—suffice it to say that the boneheads in question were, for their own reasons, busily badmouthing our home and native land as if it were the third circle of frigging hell, or some kind of 1970's-science-fiction-B-movie-dystopia or something.

Of course, being Canadian, you'll understand that I had heard the exact same kind of crap innumerable times before, and generally done my best to ignore it. But on this particular occasion, unaccountably, something just snapped. In fact, in an instant (faster than Mike Duffy on a pork chop, as we say out East), I found myself thinking: "Jesus! I wish I could get my hands on those gearboxes <u>right frigging now</u>, and maybe beat 'em into a quivering, bloody coma or something.

And then, when they came to, I wish I could stand over their badly injured carcasses and force them to read a book focusing on the many, many things about this country that are positive, rather than the usual harping on

1

and on about how the proverbial glass is one-quarter empty rather than three-bloody-quarters full! Assholes! Goddamnit!"

Of course, when I calmed down and thought about it a little more reasonably, I realized that very few worthy publications of that nature actually existed—certainly none that celebrated the (perhaps idiosyncratic) things I loved about being Canuckistani. So, I rashly decided, there and then, to get off my bone-lazy, Tortilla chip-encrusted ass and compose one.

Unfortunately, it's <u>way</u> harder than you'd think to write a book—doubly so if it's intended to be an upbeat and constructive one about Canada, 'cause you have next to no like-minded works to inspire you. Plus I kept going off on weird, trippy little tangents every time I managed the (surprisingly tedious and often tooth-pullingly painful) feat of actually cranking out a few miserable paragraphs.

So I'm afraid that what follows, Gentle Reader, inadequate as it may be, will just have to do. (If it helps, you can think of its overall mediocrity as a sly, meta-ironical commentary on the Canadian soul, or somethin'.)

The Civil Service

✦

"Bonjour! I am from the Gouvernement, and I am 'ere to 'elp you!"

The word "bureaucrat" is almost guaranteed to evoke an involuntary Pavlovian shudder from Canadians. And this is only to be expected, given the sort of experiences most of us have had with public "servants" over the years.

No, really, how many genuinely positive, satisfying interactions have you ever had with the goddamned <u>government</u>? Cast your mind back and you'll probably recall something like:

- The grueling three-month struggle you went through to convince CPP that your Old Man had actually died, and get them to change over his benefits into a chintzy $300.00 a month survivor's pension for your Mom.
- Or the soul-shredding dreariness of spending an entire Easter weekend filling out your income tax return, capped off by the apoplexy-inducing rage of discovering that you actually <u>owed</u> money this year because of all the extra friggin' overtime your boss had begged you to put in at work last summer.
- Or that baffling, barely coherent, borderline-insulting letter you got from the Employment "Insurance" weasels (eight and a half months after you'd taken the initiative and found <u>yourself</u> a new job, no thanks to those dipsticks), declaring that a $256.00 "overpayment" had been created.

So you called their 1-800 "information" number, and got the usual pass-the-buck runaround for two hours, and then you kind of snapped a little bit, I guess, and asked the third snooty French bitch they passed you off to if she could maybe write off any supposed debt against the bloated $56 billion EI surplus her department had racked up over the years, composed in part of premiums you had quite

3

arguably "overpaid" during the 23 unbroken years of employment you had put in prior to last year's layoff.

And she got all huffy of course, and hung up, so you never did find out why you owed them money in the first place (even though they deducted it from the next year's income-tax refund anyway, along with an additional penalty and compound interest).

- Or that jerk-ass customs agent who waved your family car out of the regular "long, slow, tedious" lane into the special "oh, shit" zone, and proceeded to search it for the next 75 excruciating minutes, pausing only to launch brief volleys of suspicious questions about your day's purchases and overall shopping habits, and then brusquely charge you $8.07 in extra duty and GST on the (non-Chinese, and presumably lead-free) toys you were bringing back for your nieces and nephew as X-mas presents. (All the while ignoring car after car crawling past into Canada unhindered, crammed with shifty-eyed, visibly perspiring occupants who looked like they had just blown in either from the set of Cheech and Chong's *Up in Smoke*, circa 1978, or the wild fringes of some country whose national flag depicts the beheading of an infidel.)

- Or waiting two months for the renewal passport you needed to attend your half-sister's (likely ill-advised) whirlwind-romance wedding at Sandals Freaking Jamaica. And then, at the end of it, still having to take your last remaining personal day off from work and spend it trapped in the cheerless fluorescent confines of some "Kafka Canada" limbo-of-the-lost with 80 other desperate, frustrated souls, clutching your little number-slip ("181") as if it held the cure to a loved one's leukemia.

And, finally, just barely restraining yourself from clawing through the smudged plastic barrier to throttle that fat French cow, who was hemming and hawing about your photos being a quarter-millimeter off-centre, which was clearly against "reg'lation" and would ordinarily require a reshoot, but "h'in consideration da backlog, h'I weel let h'it go."

And you, humbled by her arbitrary exercise of power on your behalf, disgusted yourself by blurting out a quick and pathetically heartfelt "Thank you," to be dismissed with a mumbled "*Bienvenue*" and a haughty flick of her indifferent eyes, sunk deep in the Franco-lard. And then you lined up at the payment desk to fork over $85.00, and thought yourself lucky to finally get out of the place at 10 to friggin' four, just as the so-old-he-probably-stormed-up-Vimy-Ridge-in-the-

Great-War commissionaire was starting to feebly shoo people out prior to closing up for the day.

•   •   •

And, when you look at it like that, I guess I see your point … dealing with bureaucrats, as a rule, <u>does</u> kinda bite. The thing is, though, that—as much as it pains one to admit it—our civil servants are actually not that bad, relatively speaking. In fact (and this could probably be added to *Roget's Thesaurus* as an example of "damning with faint praise"), our government workers are as good as any in the world.

Of course, I'm talking more about front-line service-providers here than the head-office Assistant Associate Deputy Minister nimrods in Ottawa-Gatineau—as a general rule of thumb, the closer a public servant's physical proximity to the National Capital Region, the more useless (if not actively detrimental) to ordinary Canadians he or she will be. (And, in a bizarre, totally unrelated coincidence, the closer a bureaucrat's physical proximity to the National Capital Region, the more likely it is that his or her job will be solely contingent on the ability to *parlez francais*, rather than on actual competence or ability to assist said ordinary Canadians.)

But if you look at it objectively, these unsung rank-and-filers handle a bunch of behind-the-scenes tasks that actually do add value to our lives. In fact, when a lot of stuff in this country goes smoothly—when nuclear power plants make it through one more day without melting down, and your lazy-ass brother-in-law finally gets on a subsidized carpentry course; when your Harvey's hamburger isn't made of Mad Cow, and your GST refund cheque arrives in time for St. Patrick's Day; when antibiotics don't blind your sickly, ear-infected kid, and your flight to Calgary doesn't explode on take-off—a swivel servant has likely played some part.

•   •   •

Special mention should also be made of that least appreciated and most neglected segment of our public service, the Canadian Armed Forces. Sure, we've made a show of being slightly more solicitous of them recently (i.e., since the body count in Afghanistan started rising to politically sensitive levels), but in general these poor bastards have been accorded all the respect of the ring girl at a cockfight over the past 40 years or so.

No, really! We send some of 'em up in decrepit old Sea King helicopters that were first flown by their own grandfathers back in 1963, or in fighter jets that initially proved their mettle against North Korean MIGs over Inchon.

And we launch others out to sea in fourth-rate, cut-price, have-I-got-a-deal-for-you British submarines ("the 1973 Ford Pinto of the Ocean Blue") so decrepit and unsafe that their electrical systems actually burst into flames the instant they come into contact with saltwater.

And still others wind up rolling into Taliban ambushes aboard armoured vehicles that first went into action on Juno Friggin' Beach in Normandy, with backup from the same artillery pieces that shelled Batoche during the Riel rebellion, and small arms that were in some cases seized from Montcalm's regulars on the Plains of Bloody Abraham. Oh, yeah, all together now: "There's No Life Like It and I Won't Regret The Day, When I Chose To Go The Forces Way."

So, anyway, let's take this opportunity to raise one-and-a-half cheers for public servants; we may never bring ourselves to love paying their salaries, but the poor devils deserve a shout-out for, in many ways, making possible a lot of the things we actually do enjoy about being Canadian.

Test Your Knowledge: Government and Politics!!!

Canadian politics is an endlessly fascinating subject, filled with dramatic maneuvering, passionate idealism and an ever-shifting cast of colourful characters. To measure your overall knowledge of the federal political scene, please choose the <u>one</u> response to each question that, in your opinion, most closely resembles reality.

1. This nation's politicians are:

    a) greedy, stupid jerks.
    b) pretty imperfect, but maligned more than is fair sometimes.
    c) locked in a mutually degrading co-dependence with the equally repulsive press.
    d) generally too spineless to buck "party discipline" on any point of principle.
    e) useful public servants.
    f) underpaid for a truly thankless job.
    g) unwitting puppets of the managerial elite.
    h) soulless, poll-driven moral eunuchs.
    i) reflexive spouters of hollow, mealy-mouthed platitudes.
    j) mostly trying to do their best in the face of a hyper-critical, hypocritical media microscope and a whinging, petulant electorate.
    k) a pretty poor crop, 'cause no decent person will go into politics under these conditions.
    l) all of the above.

2. Conservative Party of Canada members:

    a) love to practice goose-stepping and old-fashioned "minstrel show" routines at their constituency meetings.
    b) considered George W. Bush to be dangerously "pinko."
    c) would choose members of a "Triple E" Senate on the basis of rodeo standings.
    d) have been sucking up to Quebec a lot recently for strategic purposes but, long term, would like to see francophones placed in re-education camps until they can "talk white."
    e) want practicing "queer-osexuals" to be branded on the forehead, 'unless the sickos enjoy it or somethin'."
    f) advocate the bleaching of all immigrants before entry into Canada.

g) support capital punishment for abortionists.

h) hate all welfare recipients, unless they own a gun.

i) still pass around bootleg videos of Preston Manning describing how much he "loves that word Reeeeformmmm."

j) think Stephen Harper's gruff facade masks a sensitive, easily wounded marshmallow core.

k) distributed a written (and deeply scary) draft of their hidden right-wing agenda to all sitting caucus members in 2006. (Hint: Will involve troops. In Canadian cities. Really.)

l) have successfully tracked down and destroyed all copies of a deeply embarrassing 2002 sex tape featuring Peter MacKay, David Orchard and an unidentified goat.

m)are pretty goddamn sick of Newfoundland premier Danny Williams.

3. The Bloc Quebecois:

a) is a ridiculous, infuriating entity devoting public monies leeched from you and me to the destruction of a country that anyone else in the world would regard as a model of flexibility and accommodation.

b) would be outlawed and its leaders shot in any halfway civilized nation.

c) has inspired some sympathy for, and understanding of, Quebec's perspective in the "Rest of Canada."

d) feeds off ancient grudges and imagined or exaggerated "humiliations" like a spoiled 15-year-old, or maybe a particularly stupid Balkan demagogue.

e) has injected some novel, groundbreaking ideas into the body politic.

f) "a" and "d" are correct.

4. The NDP:

a) has many innovative, practical social and economic policies.

b) misses Bob Rae.

c) has had as significant an effect on social legislation in recent years as it did in the 1970's.

d) couldn't tell the difference between Audrey McLaughlin and Alexa McDonough, either.

e) is a dangerous, Khmer Rouge-inspired Fifth Column, thirsting for blood.

f) contains a disproportionate number of bed-wetting panty-waisters.

g) plans the unilateral disarmament of all Canadian forces (air, sea and land) as a gesture of good faith to foster dialogue with the Taliban.

h) admires Jack Layton's mustache.

i) is still deeply beholden to "Big Labour" unions, under the mistaken impression that they represent "the people."

5. The ideal Liberal Party of Canada leader for the 21st century would combine:

a) the principled decisiveness of a Paul Martin with the stirring Churchillean oratory of a Stephane Dion.

b) the cool, analytical lucidity of a Jean Chretien (in either Official Language, *bien sur!*) with the plain-spoken, salt-of-the-earth humility of a Michael Ignatieff.

c) the frugality and respect for working families' hard-earned tax dollars of a Dave ("I'm entitled to my entitlements!") Dingwall with the animal magnetism of a John Turner.

d) the bold iconoclasm of any *Toronto Star* editorialist with the steadfast, tell-it-like-it-is honesty of a Dalton ("I Won't Raise Your Taxes") McGuinty.

e) the molten sensuality of a Louis St. Laurent with the dry, Dorothy-Parker-at-the-Algonquin-Roundtable wit of a Belinda Stronach.

f) the looks, "passion," and surname of a Justin Trudeau with the good sense and decency of a John Manley.

6. Former prime minister Brian Mulroney should be visited by:

a) a Tamil Tiger hit squad.

b) avian flu-ridden chickens.

c) hungry locusts.

d) killer bees.

e) recurrent bouts of painful "jock itch."

f) the Ghost of Botched Constitutional Deals Past.

g) Sheila Copps.

h) a pack of ravening wolves.

i) his old friends Lucien Bouchard and Peter C. Newman.

j) karmic justice.

7. Many of the problems we face in Canada today can be blamed on:

a) insidious plotting by the Elders of Zion ... um, I mean "international bankers."
b) anti-Semitic crackpots.
c) the Americans.
d) worthless, parasitical welfare bums.
e) worthless, parasitical corporate welfare bums.
f) the insidious "pansy-fication" of our nation's hockey players.
g) globalization.
h) job-stealing, gibberish-spouting immigrants.
i) Kim Campbell.
j) scumbag Baby Boomers plotting to bankrupt CPP and Medicare before the rest of us get a decent kick at the can.
k) ourselves.

Answers:

1) l 2) m 3) f 4) i 5) f 6) j 7) k.

Tim's Bits

✦

"Mmmm, Doughnut ... glaghhhhhllll!"

Canadians are far from being underachievers or slouches on the global stage, whether the field of human endeavour be scientific, athletic, artistic or sex video-related.

By the same token, though, few objective observers would describe us as a "driven" people, or as being obsessed with excellence and winning at all costs—we generally do what we do in a solid, competent, workmanlike fashion, but almost never feel it necessary to strain ourselves and try for truly superior, world-beating, "Best in Show" results.

Thus, in the immense and never-ending mid-term exam that is life on planet Earth, Canadians can be said to score a pretty consistent "B+" (as indeed can this metaphor—serviceable enough, gets the point across, fairly apt; still, it lacks that extra little bit of oomph that would make it brilliant or genuinely illuminating).

This national propensity for the "good enough" is nowhere more apparent than in the economic realm—our leading businesses tend to be either uninspired harvesters of the country's bountiful natural resources (your "hewers of wood and drawers of light sweet crude") or lumbering mastodon-like occupants of a state-protected quasi-oligopoly (think your bank, cable company and cell-phone service provider; a.k.a., "Inflated, Sneaky-Ass Fee-Structures and Lackadaisical Customer Service Staff R' Us").

In neither form, though, do they exhibit the sort of nimble, bleeding-edge creativity that characterizes American entrepreneurship at its best (or, to be fair, the sort of jaw-droppingly venal, Enron-esque, sign-here-for-your-sub-prime-mortgage species of money-grubbing that characterizes it at its worst).

That's why it's so heartening to see one sector in which Canadians are clearly top-notch: I speak, of course, of the marijuana grow-op. No, no, I kid, I kid—our plucky mom-and-pop cannabis producers turn out a very fine crop, lord knows, but their industry really only approaches global excellence in parts of British Columbia, rather than across the entire country.

Nah, the business sector I'm talkin' about is even more central to daily life for most of us, nationwide, than hydroponic weed (although the two are not entirely unrelated, come to think of it): I refer, of course, to that linchpin of our domestic economy, the vital field of doughnut purveyance.

And you know as well as I do which company <u>absolutely dominates</u> that field: Tim Friggin' Hortons, that's who. Indeed, our Timmy's (according to Wikipedia, so it must be true) is responsible for stuffing over three million of its gooey lumps o' lard into Canadian gullets <u>every day</u>—no wonder we can't lose the love handles!

Oh, Tim's has its pale imitators, to be sure, but none that even approaches being a serious rival (that's right, Krispy Kreme, slink on back to your side of the border). Hell, we dote on the place so much that it has become one of our very few emotive national symbols. (Which, if you think about it, is a telling, if not faintly disturbing, insight into the Canuck psyche … particularly when you consider that this "emotive national symbol" was fully owned by "Wendy's International, Inc." from 1995 to 2006 …) (!?!)

Okay, I'll admit that the whole "patriotic icon" thing gets a bit much sometimes, what with those hokey friggin' TV commercials, and glad-handing politicians blowing in for a photo-op with "Ordinary Voters" on a thrice-daily basis during every election. And did we really need to pay X million jeezly tax-dollars to set up a Timbit counter for the troops in Afghanistan?

Be that as it may, though, there is clearly something about the place that strikes a chord in the humble Canadian soul. And, on reflection, I guess it's easy enough to see why: named for a solid, unpretentious NHL player/drunk driver; dispenser of modestly priced, tasty and unthreatening foodstuffs; welcome refuge of sleep-deprived hockey dads, conversation-starved seniors, ass-went-to-sleep-30-miles-ago transport-truck drivers (but rarely and reluctantly any cops, 'cause they resent the doughnut-munching stereotype); clean, well-lighted venue for discussions about what exactly is being done wrong this season by the local team, not to mention the manifold failings of absent friends/family members and federal/provincial/municipal governments of all stripes.

Above all, Timmy's is comfortable … none of that tiresome poser stuff you find at Starbucks, with the laptop-open-on-the-table-so-everyone-can-see-me-working-on-my-spec-screenplay-like-a-real-artist twerps ponying up $6.44 for a shade-grown-Sumatran-Peruvian-blend non-fat *Venti Frappacino Regato Grande*. Nope, at Tim's there's just regular, run-of-the-mill Joe-Lunch-Buckets and Sally-Six-Packs nursing an uncomplicated "double-double," and then rolling up the rim to win.

Nor will you find any of that fair-trade-coffee-chain freakiness at Tim Hortons, either, with the crimson-haired, Che-Guevara-T-Shirt-sporting, so-many-piercings-her-head-looks-like-a-goddamn-tackle-box barista and her organic muffins baked by Wiccan warlocks under the light of the first full moon following "Burning Man" … gimme a warm bowl of chili or Beef Noodle soup any day. (And maybe a Maple Cruller and one of them Slow Roast Beef Sandwiches while we're here, I guess.)

So, all in all, it's pretty safe to say that Tim Hortons—situated as it is at the very nexus of commerce, cuisine and social intercourse—is one of the reasons we enjoy being Canadian.

Heritage Minute: Towers of Babble

Corner of Bathurst and Dundas, Toronto, Ontario, September, 2004:

The two Rasta-men had been puzzling over their little tourist map for about five minutes, and were no closer to figuring out where they had taken the wrong turn.
"Fook it," said Long John, at last. "Let's joost ask soombuddy how to get dere."
"Okay, why not?" said Barry. Long John stepped out a little into the sidewalk, and hailed the next passerby: "Excuse me, mon, we are lookin' for the MuchMusic building ... ."

"299 Queen Street West," chimed in Barry, with his widest and most non-threatening grin. "Kin you steer us in the right direction, please, brotha?"
The man looked at them uncertainly. "Ah, sorry, no habla ... ah, I don' speak Inglese berry well, meesters ..."
Barry chuckled and gave a friendly nod. "No problem at all, mon. Sorry to botha ya!"
A second later, in turning, he caught the eye of a business-suited Asian: "Excuse m ... ."
The man instantly looked away and quickened his pace, so Long John piped up: "Sorry, could we ask ya a ...?"
"No money!" said the Asian firmly, head down and striding past.
Barry and Long John looked at each other briefly, and burst out laughing. "Lucky he didn' Kung Fu ya beggin' black ass, mon!"
"Oh, yeah, he was a real Bruce Lee son ' bitch! No money, no money!" mimicked Long John, wiping the tears from his eyes.

They took their time choosing another candidate from among the stream of pedestrians, scanning each in turn for any small sign of helpfulness or goodwill. Finally, after about ten minutes or so, Long John said, half-jokingly: "You know, I think yo' dreadlocks be causin' <u>dread</u> in the people, mon. How 'bout I just go down the end a the block and ask that fella standin' at the bus stop?"
"Might be quicker, at that," Barry agreed, and leaned against the side of a lightpole. His spirits soon brightened as he watched the bus-stop man respond positively, and at length, to his friend; then, after three or four minutes of animated discussion, they shook hands warmly, and Long John returned.
"Looking good, LJ! Whaddid he have to tell ya?"
"Fooked if I know," admitted Long John, sheepishly. "Indian guy, sounded like Apu from The Simpsons. I cood only catch mebbe one word in five of whad 'e was sayin' ... "

"Nobody in Toronna speak English, mon!" laughed Barry. "Listen, I'm tired a walkin' anyway … why don' we try 'n' grab a <u>taxi</u> down to Queen Street? Prob'ly be easier … ."

"Now yer talking … oi, we're in luck, mon, there's a cab comin' now … Give 'im a wave!"

Pause.

"That's foonny, I coulda swore 'e saw me … ah, well, surely we'll git the next one to stop, eh?"

Canadian History X

✦

"Survivor Motif or Garrison Mentality, You Be the ... ZZZZZZ"

Canadian history has a reputation for grey, soul-shriveling dullness. And, truth be told, this is not entirely undeserved—certain portions of it <u>will</u> put you to sleep faster than Extra-strength Neo-Citran mixed with warm milk, Nyquil, and a couple of ground-up Xanax tablets.

For example, next time you're suffering from insomnia, staring at the bedroom ceiling and struggling vainly to will yourself into unconsciousness, try casting your mind back to a Grade 10 class on the "BNA Act." Guaranteed it'll knock you out quicker than counting sheep (this is particularly true for those of us that grew up on a farm, for whom our wooly cousins are often more arousing than slumber-inducing).

Still, if you dig down a bit, there are innumerable facets of our national saga that can hold their own with *Desperate Housewives* for laughs, drama, and full-on "juiciness." (You'd probably remember some of them if you had actually paid attention in high school, instead of drinking yourself stupid at every opportunity and apple-bonging millions of brain cells to death with reckless abandon.)

The "King-Byng Affair," for instance, has rightly become a byword for salaciousness and titillation. As you may recall, this 1926 scandal began with a lurid whisper campaign of allegations against our "confirmed bachelor" Prime Minister of the day, the Right Honourable Mackenzie King, implicating him in an "unnatural" and "god-cursed" relationship with his long-time manservant, Gaylord Byng.

Unconfirmed rumours also circulated regarding large envelopes of untraceable "hush money" being paid to Byng's parents through certain Quebec-based ad agencies with links to the Liberal party, as well as of drunken all-night séances, during which a distraught and disheveled King begged the spirit of his late mother for "forgiveness."

These tales were, of course, never conclusively proven, and public interest gradually faded; King was therefore able to win that year's election fairly handily, and, indeed, to rack up a record six terms as Prime Minister before his retirement to Fire Island, New York, in 1948.

•   •   •

The Canadian electorate's well-known forbearance towards its political class has not been confined to Liberals, however: thus, for example, the raging and quite public alcoholism of our Tory Father of Confederation, Sir John A. Macdonald, met with limited criticism, even after his accidental shooting of D'Arcy McGee during a three-day whisky-bender in 1868. (Some historians actually go so far as to credit this incident with boosting Macdonald's popularity among Protestant voters during the 1871 election … whether or not this is true, it is clear that the Orange Order's celebrated catch-phrase "What's One Papist Potato-Muncher, More or Less?" did reflect opinion within a not-insignificant portion of the party's Ontario base.)

Similarly, the administration of Progressive Conservative prime minister John Diefenbaker was easily able to survive his rumoured assignations with Hell's Angels hanger-on Gerda Munsinger (the near-psychotic, Howard Hughes-grade paranoia, not so much), while Brian Mulroney's alleged wife-swapping with Ronald Reagan during their 1985 Shamrock Summit ("When Irish Eyes are Smiling" indeed!) met with surprisingly little public revulsion.

(Canadians instead chose to base their revulsion on Mulroney's smarminess and reckless, roll-o'-the-dice exacerbation of regional/linguistic/constitutional tensions. Plus saddling us with the GST. Oh, and the unrelenting torrents of childishly unbelievable bullshit spewed forth over the last many years to "explain" his relationship with Karlheinz Schreiber…)

This nation's history, then, is a rich pageant of fun and excitement … and, as such, is yet another reason to enjoy being Canadian.

Test Your Knowledge: Canadian Place Names!!!

Canadian place names are a fascinating, and often surprising, window into our country's past. This quiz is designed to acquaint (or reacquaint) readers with the original meanings of names we use every day, thereby deepening our collective appreciation of the rich tapestry of national history. Please keep in mind that there is only <u>one</u> correct response to each question. Good luck!

1. The city of Vancouver was named for an English naval officer, Captain George Vancouver. This intrepid explorer later went on to:

    a) have a torrid love affair with King George III.
    b) pay $300,000 for a tiny, leaky condo.
    c) open the first 87 Starbucks in the downtown core.
    d) teach English in Korea.
    e) get busted for "aggressive panhandling."
    f) harvest some really mind-bending 'shrooms.
    g) lead the Canucks to ignominious defeat.
    h) bore easterners to tears with endless prattle about the mountains, sea and "lifestyle."
    i) ram a pesky Greenpeace vessel with his flagship.
    j) sire the great-grandmother of Posh Spice.
    k) die in poverty and obscurity.

2. "Nova Scotia" is Latin for:

    a) joblessness.
    b) marginally better than New Brunswick.
    c) a tiresome abundance of colourful, folksy characters.
    d) let's try and convince them Upper Canadians that fiddle music is cool.
    e) New Scotland.
    f) New Coke.
    g) simultaneous pre- and post-industrialism.
    h) haggis-munchers.

3. The derivation of the place name "Newfoundland" is, of course, no mystery, but who actually "found" this "new land" in the first place may be a surprise. In point of fact, Newfoundland was originally discovered by:

    a) Christopher Columbus.

b) General John Cabot Trail.

c) Rudolph Hess.

d) Smokin' Joe Frazier.

e) a rogue *Who's Who in Hinterland* film crew.

f) Colombian drug smugglers.

g) drunken, smelly Vikings.

h) drunken, smelly, irrationally belligerent Irish monks.

i) nonviolent, matriarchal, environmentally conscious, Birkenstock-wearing Beothuk hunter-gatherers.

j) chance.

4. The word "Toronto" is an archaic Iroquoian term, meaning:

a) the Good

b) the Roundly Detested Everywhere Else.

c) an innocent target of small-minded jealousy and petty spite.

d) no, really, we're "world class!" Honest, we are, mister!

e) Common Sense Revolution.

f) empty pretence coupled with sneering condescension.

g) blinkered, self-absorbed ignorance hidden behind faux-sophistication.

h) damned sick of putting up with snotty little digs when we're footing the bill for the rest of you … oh, wait, I mean, "when we're already feeling bad about getting equalization money from Newfoundland in '09."

i) a moveable feast.

j) unknown.

5. "Quebec" is another place name borrowed from one of our noble First Nations. Recent linguistic research has revealed that this Algonquin term, in addition to denoting the geographical region, actually had several lesser-known meanings. From our 21ˢᵗ-century perspective, the most amusing of these alternate definitions is:

a) thin-skinned tribe with big chip on shoulder.

b) perpetual outrage.

c) a successful, long-running extortion racket.

d) effortlessly sensual, stylish women.

e) narrow-minded xenophobia.

f) Kafkaesque language cops.

g) money and the ethnic vote.

h) *Sacre Bleu*, no way those Indians can separate from us, Quebec is indivisible!

i) a distinct/unique/"special" society.

j) can't we all just (sob!) get along?

k) come on, you're just making this up to get in more of your cheap (and increasingly tiresome) Quebec-bashing.

6. "Canada" itself owes its name to an encounter in which an early explorer garbled the translation of a native word. In reality, rather than referring to the whole country, the indigenous people he met were saying:

a) How, paleface!

b) we got Marlboros, twenty bucks a carton.

c) Indians? Yeah, keep going west for another couple years or so, there, Jacques.

d) our personal failings will henceforth be your fault.

e) keep that priest away from the kids.

f) "village" or something. I forget now.

7. Likewise, the name "Ottawa" comes from an Ojibwa word indicating:

a) sloth.

b) sleaze.

c) waste and inefficiency.

d) patronage.

e) asymmetrical federalism.

f) fiscal imbalance.

g) pork-barreling.

h) pure idealism.

i) nine months of winter.

j) a local tribe.

Answers:

1) k 2) e 3) j 4) j 5) k 6) f 7) j.

Making the Best of Winter

✦

"Oh, the Weather Outside is <u>Freaking Frightful</u>"

Canada is, in countless ways, a very lucky country—blessed by nature with fertile soil and ample resources, built up by its industrious, beaver-like inhabitants into a society that is, by anyone's standards, peaceful, prosperous and tolerant (not to mention clean, reverent, and helpful to old ladies crossing the street).

Despite its manifest advantages, however, we all recognize that life in the True North Strong and Free has one major, paralyzing, deal-breaking drawback—namely, winter. (Unless you reside in the temperate "Lotusland" portion of British Columbia, of course; then, the deal-breaking drawback consists of having to fork out $800,000 for a two-bedroom starter home in the exurbs.)

Truth be told, most of us—despite our innate love of Canada, and quite contrary to the little act we sometimes put on for foreigners of being care-free, blubber-munching igloo-dwellers, inured to the cold—will find ourselves cursing this benighted land (along with whichever of our cretinous immigrant forebears chose a future in Moose Jaw rather than, say, Sydney Friggin' Australia) at least once every February.

Maybe it's the Saturday you finally give in and take the family skating on the Rideau Canal ... only to be faced with the sorrowful reality that your out-of-shape ankles haven't been atop a pair of blades in about 10 years, and began screeching for mercy two minutes after you started wobbling around the ice in the minus-35 degree wind chill.

And there're 50,000 other lame-ass SOBs who spontaneously decided to do the exact same thing at the exact same second, and are seemingly bent on getting <u>right in the freaking way</u> every time you manage to get your whole flock moving forward at the same time for two minutes in a row.

Which inevitably grinds everything to a halt, and leads to ten <u>more</u> minutes of runny-nosed whining about "I want a Beaver Tail" at five frigging

23

dollars a crack, and "I need to go pee again," and "My face is frostbitten." (And then your beloved soul-mate stops for breath and the goddamned <u>kids</u> start....)

Or maybe it's the way that snowstorms seem to hit your town with absolutely metronomic regularity from December to March, doubling the already barely tolerable one-hour commute to your (already barely tolerable) job, and turning the obligatory weekly grocery run to Loblaws into a slip-sliding, white-knuckle, *Death-Race-2000* adrenalin-fest of near-misses, sudden white-outs and barely seen threats looming out of the murk at the literal last second.

Or it could be shoveling out the end of your driveway where the city plow sealed you in for the fifth frigging day in a row. Or spending six hours of a desperately hung-over New Year's Day thawing out your Grandma's frozen water pipes with a blowtorch. Or the whole getting-up-in-the-morning-and-getting-home-from-work-in-pitch-darkness thing, where you start feeling like a coal miner in one of those Rita MacNeil songs ("oh, it's a workin' man I am, and I been down underground, and I swear to God if I ever see the sun"). And by about January 15ᵗʰ, your skin turns so pale that it's almost translucent, and you start pouring cod liver oil on the morning Weetabix 'cause your body is jonesing so bad for Vitamin D...

●   ●   ●

Anyway, you know what I'm saying: the season can kinda get you down after five, six months or so. Luckily, however, Old Man Winter does throw us an occasional bone. (Hmmmm ... is it just me, or does that sound kinda dirty?) For example, almost anyone who grew up in this weather-cursed country will treasure some fond memories of childhood "snow days."

Indeed, there are few greater joys when you're a Canadian youngster than hopping out of bed on a promising winter weekday (Monday or Friday, ideally, but they're all good), scanning the roads and skies with an appraising eye, and then super-gluing yourself to the local TV news as the cancellations are announced, concentrating all of your considerable telekinetic powers on the meat-puppet morning anchor, just <u>willing</u> him to say your school. And then the feeling of sudden, warm release (Jesus, that sounds dirty, too! Sorry!) as you hear the blessed news, and realize the day is yours!

And this delightful gift from Mother Nature is not entirely absent from the workaday adult world, either. Granted, it is fairly rare—though far from impossible—that your place of business will actually shut down for the day. Still, there are usually at least one or two mornings every winter when the correct confluence of weather-related circumstances line up in your favour and you can legitimately declare your own personal "snow day." (It helps if the police are warning people not to travel unless it's absolutely necessary … that way, your boss won't be reinforced in her belief that you're a slacker and/ or a big pussy.)

It's just this kind of unexpected day off that makes a Canadian winter bearable. Think about it—you're safe and toasty-warm inside, with (or, better, without) your loved ones, freed of all normal cares and obligations, just staring out the window and giggling like a stoned schoolgirl as the wind whips ice pellets into the bleeding faces of passers-by. Then, back to the La-Z-Boy for more bad daytime TV. Pure friggin' bliss!

◆   ◆   ◆

South-western BC is, of course, largely spared the cold-weather extremes that afflict other parts of Canada (the winter of 2008-2009 notwithstanding). Fortunately, however, there are nearly as many "snow days" in that area as anywhere else in the country. This is because any accumulation of the white stuff above one centimeter in volume will be regarded by one and all as a civilization-threatening natural disaster, and will in any case gridlock principal traffic arteries for the balance of the week, thereby making it impossible to get to work, even in the unlikely event that you want to try.

Torontonians likewise have it pretty good with respect to "snow days." Indeed, as city authorities there routinely call for an emergency armed-forces deployment whenever five centimeters or more of flurries are so much as forecast, residents feel quite justified in staying home from work for weeks at a time during an average winter. (Concerned citizens elsewhere in the country are, happily, also able to follow breathless, minute-by-minute news coverage of each year's series of "Snow-mageddons," due to the fortuitous concentration of our nation's English-language media in and around the Big Smoke.)

Conditions are, however, markedly different in our nation's third great metropolis of Montreal, the municipal workers of which are reportedly employed under an ironclad union contract absolving them from the necessity of performing any sort of labour at all, whatever the season. As a result, streets there are never plowed, sanded or salted in winter; paradoxically, though, this whimsical quirk of the distinct society yields far fewer "snow days" than one might expect.

In fact, since human activity moves into the futuristic, *Beneath-the-Planet-of-the-Apes*-style tunnel-labyrinth of Montreal's underground city each year on Remembrance Day, Montrealers are generally able to remain unaffected by surface conditions until they emerge en masse on Victoria Day (oops, my bad … of course I mean *la Fête de Dollard*, or since 2003, *la Journée nationale des Patriotes* … a provocative 'umiliation like naming a holiday for Old Vic would keep at least half of the population brooding in their catacombs 'til *St. Jean Baptiste*).

◆   ◆   ◆

"Snow days" aside, Canadians are also able to take solace in the time-honoured strategy of winging off to some sun-kissed tropical clime for a week or two in the worst depths of winter. Indeed, the anticipation of just such a break keeps many of us on the near-side of sane, and does a great deal to prevent the nation's suicide hotlines from jamming up after New Year's.

Yes, whether you're drinking yourself senseless around the pool at an all-inclusive two-star resort in Puerta Plata, leering at comely hula dancers in Waikiki, waddling up to the Lido Deck at midnight for your fifth Fun Ship buffet in 13 hours, or getting robbed and raped on an Acapulco side-street, you can rest assured that a winter sun-vacation's as Canadian as maple syrup on a Mountie.

In fact, a good case could be made that going south for a seasonal break is one of the few behavioural traits that truly unites this country's proverbial "two solitudes" … if anything, our Quebecois cousins may be even more devoted to escaping *"Mon pays, c'est hiver"* than we "My country, it's been heartbreakingly frigging cold for three months already" Anglo- and Other-phones. (This can be easily confirmed by counting the number of skintight Speedo-clad, beer-gutted males—which is to say, French-Canadians—on or near any Florida beach.)

Yup, for good and for ill, Winter binds us together and shapes us into that peculiar species of human, *"Homo Canadianis."* ("Hetero" as well.) And making the best of it is one of the reasons we enjoy being Canadian.

Heritage Minute (1): That Old-Time Religion

July, 1958, Pictou, Nova Scotia:

Dad: I seen Jeffery with that new priest again…
Mom: Where at?
Dad: Over the rink.
Mom: Yeah, Father Dan's been helping coach hockey…he's right into boys' sports, that fella, been pitchin' in with all the teams…
Dad: Huh…didn't strike me as the athletic type, first off…more of a sissy, if ya hadda asked me…
Mom: George!
Dad: (chuckling) I'm just sayin' …anyways, probably be good for Jeff to get out more, 'stead a spending so much time playing with his sisters…
Mom: Oh, yeah, he's comin' right of his shell…told me yesterday the Father wanted 'im to join the altar boys, too…(yawning)…'Night.

Pause
Dad: 'Night…

Heritage Minute (2): Religion, New and Improved
United church, Victoria, British Columbia, Sunday, September 16, 2001:

Minister: "I know how profoundly upsetting the attacks in New York have been for all of you, as they have unquestionably been for me personally, and for my family. But what should distress us all even more is the racism and intolerance that this tragedy will certainly evoke against our Muslim brothers and sisters throughout North America.

For let us not forget that Islam is a religion of peace…and our primary duty as Christians over the coming weeks, aside from the necessary task of forgiveness, will be to examine our own consciences, and ask what we have done, as a society, to provoke this kind of anger."

The Other, Better Seasons

✦

"Ha, Ha, Three Weeks of Bad Skating, I Never Heard That One Before!"

There are very, very few pleasures in the world to compare with a Canadian summer. (Okay, maybe some involving amyl nitrate poppers and a pair of high-priced Russian lingerie models, but when are you gonna luck out like that again?)

And it's little wonder—after the melancholy desolation of our near-interminable winter (see above), we Canucks fall on the warm-weather months with all the fierce desperation of starving wolves on a crippled caribou calf. No, scratch that—in point of fact, we resemble nothing more than those hardy Arctic plants that lie dormant in the tundra for 10 and a half months of the year, and then bloom madly forth for the few fleeting weeks of joyous, intense life allotted to them by Nature.

And bloom we bloody well do—in summer, Canadians' much-vaunted "caution" and "reserve" are revealed as nothing more than an artificial construct imposed upon us by the unwelcome constraints of snow and cold. Remove these winter bonds and our true selves come effortlessly to the fore—suddenly, we're out there, half-naked and happy, spiking beach-volleyballs over nets and water-skiing up rivers; guzzling pitchers of friendly late-night beer on Irish-pub patios and screeching our throats raw at rock festivals; hiking into the hills with new lovers and barbecuing big Flintstone-sized slabs of meat for supper; canoeing across lakes for the hell of it and cruising the drag in shiny convertibles.

Boring, are we? Well, come see us in July, pal—and then bugger off back to New Jersey, or wherever you're from! Eh!

•   •   •

Of course, summer, like all things in an imperfect world, is not without its minor flaws and petty annoyances. But, to Canadians' credit, we do our considerable best to ignore 'em. Doesn't matter if the temperature heats up to near-Venusian levels, with triple-digit humidex readings and month-long smog alerts. Doesn't matter if your sun-burned back has peeled off enough flesh to expose the underlying vertebrae, and you're buying Oxycontin from carnival folk to try and survive the pain. Doesn't even matter if you have to wheel an IV cart with units of whole blood around with you to drip back all the juice sucked out by the swarms of man-eating mosquitoes and mutant, piranha-like black flies that buzz in from the surrounding countryside in dense clouds whenever you poke so much as an inch of skin outside the cottage door.

Nope, none of that stuff counts at all: true Canadians will get out and enjoy summer if it's the last friggin' thing they do, 'cause they know in their bones, in the very fibre of their DNA, that another winter's comin', soon, and that it'll be just as brutal as the last one.

◆   ◆   ◆

Yup, summer is one of the things we <u>very much</u> enjoy about being Canadian. Which doesn't mean that the other two seasons should get their panties in a knot and be all jealous and shit … we love you guys, too. (Granted, it may not be the type of rapturous, full-blown passion we have for summer … probably more like the kind of subdued, minor-key affection one feels for a stepchild. But we're <u>fond</u> of you, in our own way, there's no disputing that …).

Spring, for example, is that vital, sometimes as much as three-to-four-week transition period between full-on winter and deep summer … the brief climatic window 'twixt frostbite and sunstroke, as it were. Oh, yeah, spring is always balm for the windchill-weary Canadian soul—evenings rapidly lengthen; waterfowl wing back from the Southland in honkin'-big V's; snow-banks vanish; trees bud; blood quickens; and a young man's fancy turns to Stanley Cup playoff pools … .

Sure, it's often delayed, and near-schizophrenic in its capriciousness and changeability; sure, there's a lot of rain and mud and flooded basements and such. But face it—after five months of cold-weather SADness and existential despair, we'd sell our grandmother's soul for the chance to wallow in a big puddle of spring muck.

And autumn—well autumn's awesome; peaceful, contemplative, replete with beautiful colours and salubrious temperatures … like the golden, languorous afterglow of summer's months-long orgy of amyl nitrate poppers and wild lingerie-model love-making … .

<u>Test Your Knowledge: Canadian Women!!!</u>

Canadian women are, on the whole, much less amused by the phrase "wild lingerie-model love-making" than Canadian men—indeed, many will find the attempted "joke" to be puerile, if not mildly revolting.

This quiz is designed to highlight some other basic differences between the sexes, on the way to a deeper understanding of Canadian women's needs, wants and preferences. To this end, please choose the <u>one</u> response to each question that, in your opinion, most closely reflects the truth.

1. Skills, traits or attributes that women find attractive in a man include:

    a) accurate tobacco juice spitting.
    b) that clever "pull my finger" trick.
    c) ability to quote at length from "Monty Python."
    d) honesty and sensitivity.
    e) mob connections.
    f) inordinate enthusiasm for the "Three Stooges."
    g) inordinate enthusiasm for the "Village People."
    h) opening bottles with his teeth.
    i) opening bottles with her teeth.

2. Which of these things does a woman like her partner to do on a regular basis?

    a) belch out the *Dukes of Hazzard* theme song.
    b) ogle more attractive women when he thinks she isn't looking.
    c) get loaded at parties and puke on her friend's bathroom floor, then take a swing at somebody.
    d) doze off when she's "sharing her feelings."
    e) giggle.
    f) lie around watching TV sports in his underwear.
    g) lie around watching TV sports in her underwear.
    h) give her a foot-rub.

3. In general, what do women really want?

    a) to leech off some "worker drone" until his earlier-the-better coronary, then live it up on the poor sap's pension and insurance money.

b) successful, empowering careers and a happy, fulfilling family life.

c) pitiless, emasculating revenge for millennia of patriarchy and discrimination.

d) to prattle on about nothing for hours on end while you're trying to read the paper.

e) guys who cry often and easily.

f) a Real Man practicing the philosophy of "treat 'em mean, keep 'em keen."

4. What male physical feature is most attractive to women?

a) tight, hard buttocks.

b) vacant, rheumy, bloodshot eyes.

c) ragged, poorly trimmed handlebar mustache.

d) dandruff-coated neck and shoulders.

e) luxuriant nose, back and ear hair.

f) abnormally small penis.

g) crude prison tattoos incorporating "Born to Lose," "666" and/or swastikas.

5. Most Canadian women are looking for a long-term partner who is a(n):

a) edgy drifter.

b) malleable, easily cowed "wussy."

c) knight in shining armour.

d) opinionated, stubborn loudmouth.

e) proud, purple-Mohawked proprietor of a thriving sqeegee business.

f) unkempt repository for body lice.

g) Mama's Boy.

h) responsible, soul-crushingly dull meal ticket.

i) funny, creative, faithful, gainfully employed soul mate who is willing to squash spiders.

6. Women:

a) like to run with the wolves, for some reason.

b) are naturally more cooperative and caring than men.

c) would act better than males if they were in charge.

d) are usually wanton, shameless, sexually insatiable harlots, just itching to bed the pool guy, pizza delivery man, plumber, etc., as soon as he rings the doorbell.

e) have a number of differences from men, rooted in biology and social conditioning, but are all unique individuals about whom generalizations, of any ideological stripe, would be misleading or futile.

f) are irrational, emotional, mood-swinging hormone puppets.

g) talk too damn much.

h) like drinking *pina coladas* and getting caught in the rain.

7. Good places to meet compatible women include:

a) Trekkie … sorry, "Trekker" conventions.

b) the drunk tank.

c) SM dungeons.

d) Narcotics Anonymous meetings.

e) midnight screenings of *Thelma and Louise*.

f) the *Maury Povich Show*.

g) "No Means No" consciousness-raising circles.

h) bachelor parties.

i) night classes.

j) Internet chat rooms.

8. Which of the following statements made by women to men is <u>never</u> a lie:

a) you're the best, honey.

b) that's just a myth, size doesn't matter.

c) it's okay, now there's just more of you to love.

d) yes, it's my natural colour.

e) I <u>want</u> to split the bill.

f) I don't think your mother likes me much.

g) of course he's your son.

9. Many women would welcome a threesome with:

a) unlikely porn star Ron Jeremy and sleazy "Kiss" member Gene Simmons.

b) Bret Michaels from "Poison" and aged punk rocker Johnny Rotten.

c) Gene Hackman (in one of his villainous cowboy-movie character roles, like from *The Quick and the Dead*, or *Unforgiven*) and any oiled-up Chippendale's dancer.
d) that Hurley guy from *Lost* and Michael Moore.
e) Bob Marley and Larry the Cable Guy.
f) a Somali pirate and Mick Jagger.
g) George "Dubya" Bush and Barack Obama.
h) George Clooney and Brad Pitt.
i) Saddam Hussein and Osama Bin Laden.
j) Woody Allen and Michael Jackson.
k) O. J. Simpson and Charles Manson.
l) Richard Gere and his gerbil.

Answers:

1) d 2) h 3) b 4) a 5) i 6) e 7) i 8) f 9) h.

Space

✦

"The Final Freakin' Frontier … These are the Voyages of the, etc., etc., and so forth"

You know, I taught English in Tokyo for about five years back in the 1990's. And, on balance, it was a really good experience, in a lot of ways. I was, for example, able to morph from a scruffy, out-of-control, jobless "drunk" into a well-groomed, gainfully employed, "functioning alcoholic."

I also got to pay off some fairly onerous student loans, and meet a whole lot of great people, including one Masako Aoki, the woman who would become my wife. (They may not be everyone's cup o' tea, but, for my money— inscrutable, whale-murdering Pearl-Harbor-bombers or not—there are no nicer folks in the world than the Japanese.)

As much as I enjoyed most aspects of living over there, though, there was one thing I could never adjust to—how friggin' crowded it was! Seriously, everywhere you went, hordes and throngs and conglomerations of stiffly polite little people, scurrying around bowing and jabbering and apologizing for getting in each other's goddamned way.

You've probably seen pictures of the rush-hour subways and such, but I don't know if they even do it justice. Hell, a commuter train in Tokyo makes Dr. Zhivago's cattle car to the Gulag look like a Fall Foliage excursion on the Rocky Mountaineer.

You may also have heard the typical Japanese apartment described as a "rabbit hutch." But, Lord Lifting Jesus, I'm here to tell you that any North American farmer callous enough to house innocent rabbits in conditions approximating those of a Tokyo flat'd be besieged by naked PETA protestors faster than he could say "Pamela Anderson (Lee Rock Salomon …)."

Now, I'll grant you that Japan is an extreme example, by anyone's measure. Still, it's just about as cramped and uncomfortable in every other Asian nation, rich or poor, and anywhere you care to go throughout the developing world.

Even Europe, if you've ever been, seems confined by Canadian standards—cities too crowded, passers-by too close, countryside too ordered and tamed.

Canada, in blessed contrast, has more space than anything else; certainly more than it has ever known what to do with. Now, it may not always seem like it when you're jostling through herds of business-dorks at Bay and Dundas in Toronto, or weaving a careful slalom course through the serried ranks of beggars, winos and junkies on Vancouver's Granville Street. But even our biggest cities offer <u>wayyy</u> more elbow room than those in other countries, relatively speaking, as well as easy access to the countryside whenever we get sick of being around our fellow goddamn citizens.

We locals may take this gift for granted, but it is mind-blowing for foreigners. (This is literally true—Banff residents, for example, routinely have to sidestep little puddles of gory grey matter where Asian tourists' heads have blown apart. Similarly, only about 30 percent of foreign visitors ever make it back from those Aurora Borealis tours to Yellowknife; northerners are reportedly now organizing their own trips to watch the *Scanners*-like cranial explosions.)

Wide-open space, then, is one of the reasons we should enjoy being Canadian.

Heritage Minute(s): Watching Canadian TV

New Year's Eve, 2007, Winnipeg, Manitoba:

Man: I swear to God these guys used to be way funnier…remember that fella who died a few years back, used to do Jock MacBile? I always pissed myself laughin' watchin' him!
Woman: Ah, it's almost over anyhow…hold on 'til the Chicken Cannon, then we'll click over and see if Dick Clark's still alive.

October, 1960, Halifax, Nova Scotia

Dad: If those goddamn kids don't quit their arsing around and sit still, they'll be gettin' it! Don Messer's comin' on!
Mom: You heard yer father!
Boy: Here, take yer dinky, then, ya big sook…now shush, or we'll both be in for it!

Early December, 1973, Moncton, New Brunswick

He: Jumpin' German Christ, is there nothin' on other than John and Janet Foster, gallivanting around in the backwoods?
She: Nope. I already checked the newspaper before you come in, too, and there'll be nothin' on CTV all night, neither. Why don't you go turn 'er off, and we'll play some cribbage?

Saturday morning, present day, Saskatoon, Saskatchewan

Toddler: Look, Daddy, doggy running!
Dad: Eh? Whatcha watching, there, pumpkin?
Toddler: "Li'lest 'obo!"
Dad: I'll be damned, I know this one … Hobo swims across and locks the bad guys in the cabin a that boat, eh? By Jeez, must be 20, 25 years since I seen the show…
Toddler: Finished…
Dad: Can you sing the doggy's song? "Maybe Tomorrow, I'll Try and Settle Down …Until Tomorrow, I'll Just Keep Movin' On…"
Toddler: "Ah'll Jess Key Moobin On…"
Dad: Shush, now, there's the old Spiderman *cartoon startin' … "Spiderman, Spiderman, does whatever a…"*
Toddler: Daddy, I wanna go outside…
Dad: Hold on a second, let's see what's goin' on first. Is that 'The Rhino?' Yeah, he's bustin' into the bank, see, and Spiderman's gonna swing in and ….

Cable TV

✦

"Our Boob Tube Overfloweth"

So here I am, just turned 43 years old and already a freaking dinosaur in the eyes of the younger generation.

Didn't really realize that I'd turned into Andy Rooney until about a week ago, when I was eating lunch with a couple of twenty-something co-workers. We were in the break-room, munching sandwiches and idly shooting the shit, like people do—then, for reasons that must have seemed sound at the time, I go and mention something about when the first ATMs came out, back in the early 1980s.

This little nugget stopped the conversation cold, of course—in fact, the two whipper-snappers gawped at me as if a pterodactyl penis had suddenly sprouted outta my forehead. "Uh, well, how'd you get, you know, like, money?" one of 'em finally thinks to enquire.

And I explained about the ultra-convenient way we had back then of going <u>into</u> a bank (from 10:00 to 3:00, any non-holiday weekday), filling out a withdrawal slip and waiting in a long, slow line-up to receive cash from an APM (Affectless Pink-Collar-Female-Teller, Man).

Can't say that this impressed the young fellas, really. Nor should it have—cripes, the whole process seemed pretty dumb to me even at the time. Still, lunch would've probably turned out okay if I hadn't rashly followed up by telling them about some <u>other</u> linchpins of modernity that we did without during the distant days of my dark-age youth. (Dag-nab and consarn it!)

Like how no one had a personal computer back then, let alone Internet access ("Not even <u>dial-up</u>?") … when I was in high school, we had to find pornography in "magazines," and go to a frigging "library" to plagiarize info for our term papers. (Which—at least until the advent of the first futurific *Commodore 64*s and *Wang*s—then had to be tapped out on these primitive sorta word-processor-dealies called "typewriters.")

And how, back in the day, there was no such thing as Rogers Video-on-

Demand, or DVDs from Netflix, or PVRing something so you could fast-forward through the commercials later. Hell, my family lived too far out in the Nova Scotian countryside to even get cable TV in the '80s … we considered it a major leap forward for civilization when people were first able to rent one of them new-fangled "VCRs" and some "videotapes" for the weekend, rather than being stuck with the viewing options afforded us by <u>the two English-language channels available in rural Cape Breton at that time</u>.…

♦   ♦   ♦

…Anyway, that did it … there's no way those callow pups could wrap their fragile little minds around a concept as hostile and alien as a two-channel universe. So they scurried back to their cubicles to play video solitaire and forward joke e-mails all afternoon. And I briefly cursed them under my breath, and returned to my own work-station to surf the Net until I could safely sneak out and head home.

But our little discussion came back to me that night, after dinner. (Believe I was sprawled slug-like on the sofa at the time, as is my custom.) And it got me to thinking about how much better things actually are right now in the amusing-ourselves-to-death department.

I mean, television today is so vastly superior to that of the early '80s that it might as well be a whole new medium. Back then, as I mentioned, country bumpkins like my family were stuck with either CTV (think the cheesiest, most god-awful and mind-rotting simulcast dreck, like the *Love Boat* and *Fantasy Island*) or the CBC (which, if memory serves, oscillated back and forth between the dreariest of home-grown *Road-to-Avonlea*-meets-*Pit-Pony* family fare and the mushiest of four-legs-good-two-legs-bad leftist sermonizing).

Nowadays, in contrast, anyone with a cable subscription has access to a cornucopia of quality programming that would've made my teenage head spin: *National Geographic*, *History* and *Discovery Channel* documentaries; *Comedy Network* performances from the finest American and Canadian stand-ups; *BBC, CNN* or *Fox* news and current affairs; *MuchMusic* interviews/concerts with legendary artists and rising stars, both domestic and foreign.

And, above all, complex, nuanced, envelope-pushing dramas, like *The Sopranos, Dexter, Mad Men, Six Feet Under, Breaking Bad, Rescue Me* … I mean, I hate to get all fruity on ya, but these series have at times approached the caliber of Real Art, no? (Not the sort of preening, thumb-sucking, beating-people-over-the-friggin'-head-with-its-Ponderous-Profundity wank-job "ART" beloved by Department of Canadian Heritage bureaucrats, deconstructionist professors and Toronto cocktail-party bores, either; I mean material that actually makes an effort to entertain its audience, while at the same time attempting to reflect humanity in all of its self-contradictory freakiness.)

◆   ◆   ◆

Watching the Idiot Box isn't a particularly prestigious pastime … but, on a pitch-dark, life-threateningly cold winter's night, when work/family and all their attendant, incessant, spirit-eroding bullshit have left us too wrung-out to even <u>try</u> anything constructive, I think a lot of us would agree that cable television is a comfort.

And, as such, I guess it's one of the (secret) reasons that we enjoy being Canadian.

<u>Test Your Knowledge: Television!!!</u>

We may not like to admit it, but most of us have watched <u>way</u> too much television over the years. This quiz is designed to see what you know about the medium—to measure your TV IQ, as it were. In order to do so, please choose the <u>one</u> best response to each question.

1. Many popular series from past decades live on today in syndication, giving fans a chance to catch favorite episodes again and again. One familiar plot-line typifying the timeless spirit of a classic program involves:

    a) Mr. Roper discovering that Jack is actually heterosexual, recruiting Keanu Reeves as girls' replacement roommate.

    b) Hawkeye Pierce self-righteously defending UN-approved police action in Korea, sending lightly wounded teenage "malingerer" back to the frontline to resist Commie aggression.

    c) Partridge Family being beaten to a bloody pulp by Hells Angels at Altamont.

    d) Gilligan moving in with the Professor after Skipper has one too many bouts of "sleepwalking."

    e) Jan Brady lifting an ounce of pot from Greg's stash, planting it in Marcia's (Marcia, Marcia, <u>Marcia's</u>) school locker, making anonymous call to principal.

    f) George Jefferson counseling maid Florence on the need to cut "honkies" a little slack.

    g) Potsie snapping, going on a bloody murder-suicide rampage at "Arnold's" while Fonzie cowers in the men's room.

h) Dr. Johnny Fever at last revealing that he is a "deep cover" narcotics agent, slapping the cuffs on Andy and Venus Flytrap.

i) Fred Flintstone enlisting the Great Gazoo's help to steal *Honeymooners* scripts.

j) Mary Tyler Moore whining "Mr. Gra-aa-ant!," breaking down in tears, being patronizingly let off the hook.

2. One thing that has never, ever been seen on TV is a(n):

a) white-trash punch-up on *Jerry Springer*.

b) Asian woman news anchor.

c) no-nonsense black female judge.

d) embarrassingly unfunny, painfully dragged-out sketch during the last half-hour of *Saturday Night Live*.

e) *Seinfeld* episode in which the core characters brighten their pointless, unproductive, hateful little lives with snide remarks and entirely unwarranted smugness.

f) prisoner interaction with pronounced homo-erotic undertones on *Oz*.

g) intelligible Ozzy Osbourne.

h) Sarah Palin guest appearance on *30 Rock*.

i) enraged *Dr. Quinn, Medicine Woman* leading townsfolk on a reprisal raid against "thievin' redskins."

3. TV networks sometimes film programs that they later decide not to broadcast. In Canada, this has included episodes of:

a) *The Friendly Giant* (1971: "Jerome the Giraffe Accidentally Bites Rusty's Bag").

b) *The Beachcombers* (1973: "Nick and Jesse Take On a Cabin Boy").

c) *The Red Green Show* (1992: "Careful With that Axe, Eugene").

d) *Street Legal* (1994: "Barr, Rabinovitch and Tchobanian Finally 'Do It,' While That Vixen Olivia and her Visibly Tumescent New Boyfriend Watch").

e) *Da Vinci's City Hall* (2006: "Dominic Completes One Underwhelming Term as Mayor, Then is Appointed to the Senate by Paul Martin").

f) *Mr. Dressup* (1981: "Finnegan 'Goes to Live in the Country'").

g) *Mr. Dressup* (1982: "Casey Is Deeply Traumatized by Contents of the 'Tickle Trunk'").

h) *Little Mosque on the Prairie* (2008: "Imam Rashid's 'Extraordinary Rendition' to Syria").

i) *Little Mosque on the Prairie* (2009: "Imam Rashid's Return Home and Subsequent Multimillion-dollar Lawsuit Against the Federal Government").

j) *The Lens,* on CBC Newsworld (2007: "Beyond the Red Wall: The Persecution of *Falun Gong*").

4. In a related vein, the CBC is known to maintain an archive of programs that have already aired once, but which will likely never be rebroadcast. This includes:

a) that *King of Kensington* episode where Larry joins the Jewish Defense League and ends up breaking the legs of a suspected Nazi war criminal.

b) the 1972 *Wayne and Shuster Comedy Special* in which Progressive Conservative party leader Bob Stanfield tries desperately to appear hip by dropping awkward references to "reefer" and repeatedly asking the audience to "Sock it to me!"

c) Mary Lou Finlay's final appearance on *The Journal*, which ended with her flipping out and clawing a long, red scratch across Barbara Frum's smug, taunting face.

d) a 'Town Hall' segment from *The National* that <u>didn't</u> immediately degenerate into sterile ideological axe-grinding and smarmy, self-important soliloquies from *soi-disant* intellectuals in love with the sound of their own voices.

e) a fairly recent Thursday-night airing of *The National*, which was disrupted when a thick cloud of pompous self-satisfaction temporarily obscured the entire "At Issue" panel.

f) Tommy Hunter's famously profane tirade against "filthy hippies," back in 1970.

g) the 1996 Christmas special on which Rita MacNeil and Anne Murray shared a deep tongue-kiss.

h) the "heartwarming" period drama during which Gordon Pinsent's acting talent finally gave up and oozed out of his left ear.

i) that whisky-fuelled donnybrook during *The Irish Rovers*.

j) the notorious *Front Page Challenge* on which Pierre Berton can be seen rolling a nice, fat joint.

5. Similar "forbidden episodes" on other Canadian networks include:

a) *MuchMusic* (1985: Erica Ehm disappears into "Loverboy's" tour bus for the balance of her shift, leaving a nonplussed J. D. Roberts to fill 45 minutes of dead air).

b) *Canada's Next Top Model* (2007: heterosexual male is accidentally booked as guest judge, throwing the proceedings into turmoil).

c) *Canadian Idol* (2006: newest winner vanishes into obscurity before the final credits have even stopped rolling).

d) *Trailer Park Boys* (2003: "Shirtless Randy" skins Frank and Gordon, the "Bell Beavers," then trades their pelts to Bubbles for a bag of dope and two cheeseburgers).

e) *Corner Gas* (2009: "Hillbilly Heroin" cuts a grim swathe through Dog River).

f) *SCTV* (1980: Bob and Doug McKenzie get hammered on Newfoundland Screech, with messy results).

g) *Night Heat* (1991: Detectives O'Brien and Giambone go undercover in a Jamaican drug posse).

h) *CRTC Hearing* (2009: network mouthpieces cry poor and beg for hefty "carriage fees" to be inflicted on Canadians).

6. My favourite kind of TV commercial involves:

a) earnest mother-daughter discussions about "freshness."

b) an old crone who has fallen and can't get up.

c) "cool" teenagers replying "Duhhhh!" to an adult's question.

d) mysterious blue liquid being poured onto diapers.

e) starving African children being used to shill for donations.

f) an iconic Baby Boomer rock standard being prostituted to sell cars, computers, mutual funds, etc.

g) anything that slices, dices <u>and</u> makes Julienne fries.

h) cute talking animals, babies, baby animals, etc.

i) healthy, happy, sexy young people holding (but if you watch closely, never actually being allowed to drink from) beers.

j) the ingenious "clapper" device.

k) that adorable "Canadian Tire couple" from a few years back.

l) any McCain pizza ad ('cause they're all so clever!)

m) those "good" American ads that our government perversely persists in blocking during each year's *Super Bowl*.

n) clichéd, self-congratulatory rants about how "I. Am. Canadian."

o) CBC's familiar loop of demographic-friendly products and services (Grey Power car insurance, Easy Entry bathtubs, Depends adult diapers, CHIP reverse mortgages, and so forth).

p) none of the above.

7. My favourite TV-related activity includes:

    a) getting really baked and laughing my ass off at the losers on *Intervention* and *Celebrity Rehab*.
    b) eating bowl after bowl of "Sugar-Frosted Flakes," watching frenetic, epilepsy-inducing cartoons, popping Ritalin.
    c) cheering 14 hours of NFL football while swilling a "two-four" of beer, then abusing the wife until I pass out in my own feces.
    d) actually locating a music video on MTV.
    e) using my remote control to zap through channels at the speed of a strobe light.
    f) guffawing at piñata and nun-chuk accidents, baseball groin-hits, farting dogs, wedding mishaps, etc., on *America's Funniest Videos*.
    g) trying to figure out what the hell is happening on *Lost*.
    h) hanging on every word of exciting acceptance speeches during five-hour-long awards show.
    i) asking anyone within earshot of my La-Z-Boy how a CBC schedule padded out with *Wheel of Fortune*, *Jeopardy*, *Coronation Street* and endless Adam Sandler movies constitutes "telling Canadian stories to Canadians."
    j) masturbating to Ultimate Fighting cage matches on Spike TV.
    k) counting the inordinate number of Jewish-looking names in show credits for my "white nationalist" blog.
    l) fantasizing about slapping the sunglasses off of David Caruso's talent-less face.
    m) fantasizing about killing "Jim" from *The Office*, then abducting that "Pam" chick.
    n) wistfully enjoying a *Simpsons* re-run from the glory days, while bemoaning the comparative suck-itude of all post-1998 episodes.
    o) sneering at the eunuch who plays "Lynette's" husband on *Desperate Housewives*.

8. Television networks broadcast numerous movies, either created especially for them or purchased from a film studio because of their mass appeal. One movie plot that would <u>never</u> make it to air involves a:

    a) pair of comically mismatched cops battling crime and police department bureaucracy, trading wisecracks.

b) maverick loner cop defying his hidebound superiors to solve a crime.

c) group of really cool criminals outwitting stupid and/or corrupt cops.

d) high school loser exhibiting hitherto-hidden courage, impressing girl of his dreams.

e) fiendishly intelligent psychopath butchering a bunch of people in imaginative ways.

f) lowly young employee impersonating an executive, taking the corporate world by storm.

g) really different man and woman initially hating each other, then falling in love.

h) plucky person fighting a newly fashionable disease, learning about his/her self, dying bravely.

i) plucky woman killing her abusive mate, beating the murder rap slapped on her by a sexist society.

j) selfish teacher seducing a teenage boy, persuading him to kill her husband.

k) wacky gang of Iranian secret policemen and their campaign against Zionist-inspired Kurdish separatists.

9. TV is a:

a) cultural wasteland.

b) tool used by the liberal media elite to spread immorality, permissiveness and disrespect for free enterprise.

c) tool used by our corporate masters to spread hollow, wasteful consumerism and coded racism/sexism.

d) great way to learn about life.

e) time-effective way for Paris Hilton to find a new BFF.

f) useful baby-sitter.

g) direct cause of violence.

h) comfort to the sick and shut-in.

i) medium that (sometimes disturbingly) reflects, and to a degree creates, contemporary North American culture.

j) trivial non-issue only idiots would get worked up over.

k) could be "i" or "j." Or, cripes, "all of the above" … whadda I look like, a goddamn Poindexter or somethin'?

Answers:

1) j 2) i 3) j 4) d 5) h 6) p 7) i 8) k 9) k.

PET Sounds

✦

"They Haunt Us Still"

Although certain snide foreign sources will no doubt continue to insist otherwise, the term "Greatest Canadian" was in fact coined well before 2007, when its surprise victory in the "Funniest Oxymoron in the Entire Universe" competition left all of Los Angeles abuzz. (An oxymoron, as you will recall, is an inherently self-contradictory formulation, like "jumbo shrimp," "military intelligence," "progressive conservative," "happily married," "Middle East peace," etc.)

Indeed, this amusing phrase can be traced back as far as 2004, when it appeared as the title of a 12-episode (!?!) CBC TV series in which various domestic "celebrities" debated the identity of Canada's Niftiest and Most Exemplary citizen. (Awful sorry you missed that whole exercise, aren't ya?)

Spoiler alert! Turns out that Tommy Douglas was the Greatest Canadian. (Remember, though, that this was based on the votes of CBC viewers; opinions would no doubt vary in the "under 50" demographic, as well as among the sizeable portion of our populace who would rather put their own eyes out with a feces-smeared knitting needle than watch this nation's beloved public broadcaster.)

Now, Tommy D. is not a bad choice, I guess (although my money was on sprinter Ben Johnson the whole time), especially when his merits were so forcefully outlined by scrumptious "celebrity" advocate George Stroumboulopoulous, with that tight black T-shirt and those dreamy hipster eyes … and, oh, that little soul-patch … mmmm… .

…But whatever the Father of Medicare's undeniable virtues, I must admit to having been more persuaded by the Mother Corp's resident High Forehead, Rex Murphy, who mounted a pretty effective argument in favour of Pierre Elliot Trudeau. (At least I think he did … word to the wise: hit "Closed Caption" on your remote whenever Mr. Polysyllabic-Rhodes-Scholar-with-a-

Thick-Newfoundland-Accent opens his considerable yap, and you'll do <u>way</u> better in following along.)

And, whatever you or I may think of the actual <u>desirability</u> of Trudeau's legacy (or of the actual <u>desirability</u> of luscious Strombo relative to that of Halloween-Ghoul-Asaurus Rex), it's hard to deny that the fella had a far "Greater" impact on us all, for better <u>and</u> for worse, than Tommy Douglas or anyone else you care to mention.

This accounts for PET's continued, and remarkable, emotional resonance, particularly for Canadians of a Certain Generation (rhymes with "Maybe Doomers"). Indeed, you will likely remember the nation's somewhat over-the-top reaction back in September 2000, after Pierre shuffled off this mortal coil to rejoin his compatriots on Mt. Olympus—the long lines of shaken, teary-eyed citizens spontaneously materializing in downtown Ottawa; the somber, sonorous tones of pundits and politicos reminiscing about our nation's long-gone glory days; the small children brought to gaze in awe on Dear Leader's body as it lay in stuffed, Lenin-like state on Parliament Hill … .

Yup, it was all pretty goddamned moving. So much so that many Albertans (not to mention Quebecers, and fairly sizeable chunks of the population in each of the other provinces and territories) had to be physically restrained from <u>moving</u> to a less misguided country, like maybe Zimbabwe, and/or from flying to Ottawa themselves and driving a precautionary stake through Trudeau's shriveled, black, tyrannical heart to make sure the evil prick would never return. And maybe another stake through the addled brain of any dumb sumbitch who would drive his kid 10 hours from Sault Ste. Marie to mourn the old bastard's long-overdue departure for Hell.

◆   ◆   ◆

Now, as I've already hinted, I fell more in the latter camp than the former. Truth be told, I was never a huge fan of our sainted PET when he was PM, and was at first more or less indifferent to his passing (until those throngs of weepy, corpse-gawking Boomers started to show up on the Hill, at which point I began to recall some of my own long-buried, and exceedingly ungenerous, feelings about the guy).

See, I was born in '66, so I'm a little too young to remember any of the good times. I mean, Trudeau-mania <u>sounds</u> like a hoot: mini-skirted teeny-boppers squealing 'til they wet themselves 'cause they had just scratched a Mountie who had touched some flunky who had brushed against the sleeve of the Great Man's friggin' Nehru jacket, or whatever. And the cool, pirouetting-behind-the-stuffy-old-queen, sliding-down-banisters, rappin'-with-John-and-

Yoko-about-Peace-and-the-Just-Society Philosopher King of the first few years seems, like, groovy, ma-aa-ann!

But, unfortunately, my earliest impressions of the man are from the mid-70's—thus, in my mind, *cher Pierre's* image is indelibly bound up with long, grey years of stagflation and unemployment, not to mention duplicitous wage-and-price-controls ("zap, you're frozen") and the borrow-and-squander financing of ever-expanding, largely uncalled-for public "services."

Throw in an inexplicable (but nonetheless vile and stomach-turning) fondness for mass-murdering Marxist dictators, season with some arrogant shrugging and sneering and cocky gunfighter posturing, add a pinch of fuddle-duddling and flipping off of the actual working Canadians who had to bankroll his grand visions, and what's not to dislike? (Of course, to be fair, Pierre-O also made possible the edifying Seventies spectacle of First Spouse Margaret, whose bi-polar Studio 54 crotch-flashing and Rolling Stones-boning did so much to lift Canadians' spirits during the latter part of that difficult decade.)

So, in a nutshell, I guess I've always regarded Trudeau as—how does one put this delicately?—as a bit more of a <u>dick</u> than would people with a longer frame of reference and, perhaps, a different set of ideological biases. At the same time, though, I continue to maintain that PET's legacy of Dystopian Trudeaupianisms richly merits its inclusion on any half-baked list of "things to enjoy about being Canadian."

The reason, of course, is the conspicuous, unequivocal <u>failure</u> of so much of what he tried to do, from the National Energy Policy to the Foreign Investment Review Agency; from free-and-easy UIC to devil-may-care deficits; from an Official Bilingualism equally unwanted by both "Founding Nations" to the emasculation of our "justice" system; from the forced collectivization of Ukrainian farms to the exile of the *kulak* stratum of peasantry to camps in Siberia … .

…Well, all right, I suppose I'm getting a little *National Post* here. But still, it can't be denied that a fair percentage of Trudeau's policy prescriptions (a.k.a., "mush-headed crypto-socialist claptrap") have not only failed, but <u>been seen to have failed</u> by a significant minority, maybe even a critical mass, of us … they are, in a very real sense, a living, cautionary example of what doesn't work and what ought never to be repeated.

So, no matter how bleeding-hearted and candy-assed we may collectively remain in a lot of respects, Canadians have at least gained a degree of healthy skepticism about statist meddling, and a much deeper appreciation of the Immutable, Age-old Law of Unintended Consequences. And we have the Great Helmsman Himself to thank for imparting these valuable lessons.

So, RIP PET. And *merci*, you magnificent, misguided son of a bitch!

Heritage Minute: Agreeing to Disagree

G8 protests, downtown Ottawa, Ontario, June, 2002:

The police sergeant tried again: "Okay, everybody, we're gonna need you to clear the street now! Please disperse!"
"This is a peaceful demonstration, man!"
"Dissent!"
"Hey, hey, ho, ho, globalization's got to go, hey, hey…"
"The people, united, will never be defeated!"
Marcel, now at the front of the crowd, got up right in the face of one of the younger cops, and shouted "Go lick George Bush's boots, you corporate tool!" *Jeers and catcalls of approval rose from the protestors behind him.*
"Okay, cool down now, no need for that," *soothed an older officer, just to the right of Marcel's initial target.*
"Blow me, pig!" *responded Marcel, staring him straight in the eye. The older cop looked away, and seemed to slump a little in tacit defeat.* "Stop resisting," *he said in a resigned voice.*
"Eh?" *said Marcel.*
"Stop resisting!" *the younger cop joined in, more loudly, and shoved Marcel a little off balance with the butt of his baton.*
"I'm not resis …!"
"STOP RESISTING!!!" *screamed the older officer as he span around to kick Marcel in the ankle.*
"Owww, fuck!" *Marcel snapped forward in pain: he didn't even realize the first baton had hit his skull until seconds later, when someone heavy was kneeling on his head and mashing the left side of his face into the asphalt.*
"Stop resisting! If you don't stop resisting, we will be forced to use a TASER to ensure immediate compliance!"
Blood dribbled out of Marcel's mouth as he tried desperately to speak; there was just time enough to burble: "No, please, I'm n…" *before the first 50,000-volt charge of electricity convulsed his entire body.*

Poutine

✦

"Charging to 300 … And, Clear!"

Given the delicacy and nuanced thoughtfulness with which I have hitherto approached all matters pertaining to French Canada, it will doubtless surprise readers to learn that I—like many *maudits anglais*, one suspects—sometimes get a little annoyed with our Quebecois brothers and sisters.

And who could blame us, really? I mean, hell, I'm in my early 40's right now, so our erstwhile *Belle Province* has been bleating and belly-aching and saber-rattling and threatening to take the kids and go home to Mother (to mix a metaphor or three) for literally as long as I can remember.

That being said, there is one big benefit the "Rest of Canada" has gotten from Quebec that very nearly makes up for the many dreary decades of constitutional-angels-dancing-on-the-head-of-a-frigging-pin, undeserved "equalization" payments, boring-ass-Jeffery-Simpson-columns ("Whither Confederation?: Part XXXII"), and bilingual labels that you always turn to the French side first when you're trying to figure out how long to microwave your goddamned Campbell's Chunky Soup.

That one big boon is, of course, poutine. This is not, I hasten to add, because poutine is a particularly healthful addition to our collective Canadian diet; in fact, if you concentrate hard enough after eating some, you can sometimes actually feel your arteries clogging up and congealing into a solid lump of plaque as your body labours at digesting it.

Instead, it is because of that most basic of the five senses, Taste. Seriously, what other "comfort food" could be … errrr, well, as comforting? Golden-brown chunks of French-fried, carbohydrate-rich potatoes, saturated in tangy cheese curds and sodden with glorious, glutinous gravy—season vigorously with salt, and you've got one hell of a fine meal.

This noble dish lifts us up when we're feeling blue; restores warmth to our hypothermic bodies when we stumble in from a wholesome Canadian afternoon of pond hockey, Skidooing or snow-shoveling; leaps instantly to

51

the rescue in our hung-over guts, coating the tender, liquor-ravaged tissues in soothing balm and magically absorbing the harmful toxins from yesterday's dimly remembered debauchery; and in a pinch, makes a serviceable caulking agent for one's bathtub.

Poutine, then, is the greatest—nay, the most quintessential!—Canadian food (with an honourable mention to that old stalwart, Kraft Dinner). And, as such, it certainly qualifies as a good reason to enjoy being from here.

Test Your Knowledge: Good Health Habits!!!

Good physical health is almost a prerequisite for a happy, productive life. This quiz will help you to identify habits that may be negatively affecting your overall well-being, and acquaint you with other practices that serve most people much better. To this end, please pick the <u>one</u> response to each question that most closely reflects your own likely reaction, attitude or experience.

1. For breakfast, the most important meal of the day, I usually have:

    a) a can of Coke, maybe a bag of chips or a KitKat if I have time.
    b) a couple shots of vodka so's I can stop shaking long enough to drive to work.
    c) three or four DuMauriers.
    d) two fried eggs, bacon, glass of melted Crisco.
    e) whatever I can scavenge from the dumpster out back of "Denny's."
    f) carefree, unprotected sex with whoever's lying around the apartment that morning.
    g) fresh fruit, whole wheat toast, skim milk.
    h) my Librium melted into an omelet by the nurse.

2. I go to a doctor or medical clinic:

    a) every six months for a checkup.
    b) if my track marks get infected.
    c) to get mysterious rashes in my nether regions checked on.
    d) whenever the judge orders a blood test.
    e) to try to swipe a prescription pad.
    f) 'cause I get a kick outta smearing infectious mucous on back issues of *Newsweek*.
    g) to see if I can trump up a lawsuit.

3. I keep in shape by:

    a) playing bingo.
    b) splitting hairs.
    c) jogging to the 7/11 for smokes.
    d) hauling my empties back to the liquor store.
    e) sexually harassing subordinates at work.
    f) bench-pressing Norman Mailer novels.
    g) going to the "Y" two or three times a week.
    h) snatching purses.
    i) barking and chasing cars.

4. I shower:

    a) pretty much every day.
    b) on a drafty stage in front of a crowd of drooling, drunken perverts.
    c) every Wednesday and Saturday, unless the screws throw me in "solitary" for some reason.
    d) so my husband won't find out.
    e) in a raincoat.
    f) high-pitched, keening invective on passersby who decline to donate any "spare change."

5. A healthy dinner for me would consist of a:

    a) skinless chicken breast, brown rice, steamed vegetables.
    b) Bacon Double Cheeseburger, large fries, Triple Thick chocolate milkshake.
    c) handful of amphetamines.
    d) bowl of salt moistened by grease squeezed from "extra crispy" Kentucky Fried Chicken skin.
    e) medium-rare filet mignon, foie gras, chocolate mousse, cigar, eight or nine tumblers of Scotch.
    f) 40-ouncer of rum, two-liter bottle of diet Pepsi, gram of hash.
    g) casserole comprising something old, something new, something borrowed and something blue.

6. If you are diabetic, you should avoid:

    a) salt.
    b) sugar.

c) tofu.

d) Jehovah's Witnesses.

e) that freakin' *Family Circus* cartoon in the newspaper.

f) employment in the telemarketing field.

g) bus station toilets.

h) doomsday cults.

i) "b" and "e," though a defensible argument could be mounted for most of them.

7. I usually sleep:

a) between seven and eight hours a night, maybe a little more on holidays.

b) with one eye open.

c) in a crime- and pestilence-ridden hobo jungle down by the train tracks.

d) with the fishes.

e) in my comfy, satin-lined coffin, until dark.

f) with syringe-swapping prostitutes.

8. Many well-known adages contain a pithy sort of folk wisdom pertaining to health. Which of these responses best sums up your own philosophy?

a) live fast, die young, leave a beautiful corpse.

b) silly rabbit, Trix are for kids.

c) one drink is too many, a thousand not enough.

d) tune in, turn on, drop out.

e) leggo my Eggo.

f) we're here, we're queer, get used to it!

g) "9/11" changed everything.

h) acid is groovy, kill the pigs.

i) bro's before ho's.

j) Death to America!

k) Git 'r Done.

l) in the desert, you can remember your name, 'cause there ain't no one for to give you no pain.

m) the pump don't work 'cause the vandals took the handle.

n) no matter how you shake and dance, the last drop always goes down your pants.

o) these sayings are either incoherent, irrelevant or, at best, logically unprovable.

Answers:

1) g 2) a 3) g 4) a 5) a 6) i 7) a 8) o.

Gender Equity

◆

"That's Not Funny! Despite Some Significant Advances in Recent Years, Much More Needs to be Done Before Women, yada, yada, yada…"

According to the disturbingly intense, lightly mustachioed Indigo Girl who taught me first-year sociology, Canadian society is a nasty, narrow, socially constricted place, with females apparently forbidden by law from setting foot in high school math classes, corporate boardrooms, or the stuffy gentlemen's clubs in which we patriarchs nurse our snifters of brandy and discuss ways to more effectively exploit "darkies," despoil nature and generally grease the wheels of capitalism with the blood of the workers.

I also seem to recall that married women are forcibly confined to the home as unpaid domestic drudges and baby-making brood mares (oh, wait, that's scheduled for the near-future, as per Margaret Atwood's *The Handmaid's Tale*. My bad!) But, to be honest—and this will disappoint the 80 percent of my teachers, professors and bosses over the years who have been female—I can't say that I've ever really bought into the whole femi-commie narrative of gyno-oppression.

Yeah, sure, men and women have their beefs with each other, and will no doubt continue to do so until the NDP is elected to federal office and acts on its long-standing policy commitment to augment the fluoride in municipal water supplies with powdered estrogen.

And, as noted in the Introduction, it's way more fun for a lot of people to bitch and moan and get all righteously indignant about how the proverbial glass is a little bit empty rather than mostly full. (It's mostly full of one of them girly drinks, like a Cosmopolitan or whatever. Oh, you like that, baby? Lemme buy you another one … mmmm, yeah… .)

But when you come right down to it, things are a helluva lot better for women in Canada than in most of the world (unless you're fond of grinding poverty, female circumcision at puberty, "honour" killings and/or wearing a big black sack every time you venture out of doors), and they're much improved from what they were here even a few decades ago.

Are Canadians one big happy pig-pile of neutered, ambidextrous (wait, I just looked that up—I mean "androgynous") chuckleheads, then, with no inter-gender-ational frictions, grudges or resentments?

Obviously not, Smiley McDolphin! In fact, there will continue to be a fair degree of conflict and tension between men and women for as long as nature insists on wiring the sexes so very, very differently. And, crucially, for as long as <u>people in general</u>—regardless of their sex, race, colour, creed or hockey-team affiliation—continue to be clumsy, fickle, self-centred dipsticks who screw each other over constantly, by mistake and design. (That's right, Heather Mills, I'm looking at you.)

So, rather than getting all bent out of shape about it, let's embrace our common humanity and admit that we are <u>all</u> assholes, deep down. And then get back to enjoying male-female differences the way the Good Lord intended—in the sack, as part of some primal, grunting, sticky-with-sweat monkey-love.

Which, in a round-about way, brings us to:

(Definitely Not) Jane Taber's Hot and Not: Canadian Women

<u>Nelly Furtado</u> --- flat midriff-baring, faux-promiscuous girl; Hot!

<u>Slutty, Kelly-Bundy-lookalike teens hanging around the mall</u> --- sexy, but (despite your occasional idle fantasy) hardly worth going to jail for; Not.

<u>Mildly exotic visible-minority co-anchor chick on your local newscast</u> --- Hot (if you can get past the painfully-forced-banter-with-weather-and-sports-guy thing).

<u>K.D. Lang</u> --- Not.

<u>Fake Lesbians in any Porno Film, Whether Soft- or Hard-Core</u> --- Hot.

<u>Wendy Mesley</u> --- used to be Hotter, 'til Peter Mansbridge sapped her life-force and gave her cancer. Possibility that she might show up at your place of business with a *CBC Marketplace* camera crew and ask embarrassing questions is also a negative; Not.

<u>Jan Wong</u> --- hard and mean in a Black-Widow-Spider, snitching-to-the-Maoist-secret-police, two-faced-laugh-at-your-jokes-during-lunch-and-then-skewer-you-publicly-in-her-frigging-column kind of way; Not.

<u>Shania Twain</u> --- Oh, God, yes, Hot!

<u>Margaret Atwood</u> --- Not.

<u>Luba Goy from *Royal Canadian Air Farce*'s impression of Margaret Atwood droning on about feminism</u> --- funny as hell, but even more Not.

CTV Medical Specialist and Courageous Breast Cancer Survivor Dr. Marla Shapiro --- Hot.

Jane Taber herself --- hardest-working woman in show business, what with the newspaper column, *Question Period* gig, and ubiquitous "talking head" appearances on every single CTV program currently on the air, including *Degrassi: The Next Generation* and the national anthem sign-off after the late show … just squeaks in on the Hot side of the ledger.

Valerie Pringle --- preternaturally comfortable in her own skin, surprisingly well-preserved; Hot.

Inuit Throat Singers --- ???Not!?!?

Raging Grannies --- no, you sick bastard! Why would you even … ?

ET Canada hostess Cheryl Hickey --- oh, yeah, Hot!

Avril Lavigne --- nah, not really, don't see it; Not.

Maude Barlow --- Christ, no!

Celine Dion --- seems like a nice enough woman, actually, but nonagenarian husband and that *Titanic* tune weigh heavily against her; Not.

CBC Weather-Balloon and Championship Curler Colleen Jones --- nope; far too maniacally cheerful at an ungodly hour of the morning to be Hot. Plus that whole shrieking-like-a-banshee-being-boiled-alive-in-molten-sewage-when-she's-curling factor. Plus the fact that she curls. And works for the CBC; Not.

Model from Late-night Commercial for Live Singles Chat Line (Try it for Free) --- sexy as all get out, but, at $2.99 a minute, I think Not.

Pre-Cambrian Sex Therapist Sue Johanson --- Not.

Dazed, bow-legged MILF in "Cialis" commercial --- Hot.

Rona Ambrose --- has had an oddly appealing waif-like air of vulnerability since her ignominious flame-out as Environment Minister … also, Great Hair; Hot.

Belinda Stronach --- endlessly entertaining, fabulously wealthy, flighty and capricious; the blondly ambitious Paris Hilton of Canadian politics (oh, I forgot, she's bored with politics now … I mean "of Canadian business." And "charity malaria nets"). Gets bonus Hotness points for having driven poor Peter MacKay to give his famous standing-in-a-Nova-Scotia-field-with-a-borrowed-dog breakup speech (still the most side-splitting moment in Conservative party history, to date), and for having busted up Tie Domi's marriage. Would be Hot if she possessed a human soul and/or principles; as it is, Not.

Marge, Princess Warrior --- neither Hot nor, in retrospect, all that amusing.

Chantal Hebert --- astute analytical mind, excellent writer in both official languages; would be Hot if she didn't remind you of your high school gym teacher; Not.

Christie Blatchford --- also a very fine reporter, but, sadly, makes Chantal Hebert look like Scarlett Johansson; Not.

Karla Homolka --- Hot (although you would never admit it out loud to anyone); will be considerably Hotter in a few years, when she's roasting in the fiery pits of Hell.

Barbara Amiel --- what is she, like, 110? Still, she appears to be held together by the same space-age American technology pioneered by Cher; Hot, God help me!

Rebecca Eckler and Leah Maclaren --- Not (even if you could somehow tell them apart).

Erstwhile Biker Chick and Cleavage-flaunting Foreign-ministerial Arm-candy Julie Couillard --- career- (and potentially life-) threatening, but; Hot.

Kim Cattrall --- Not, for many years now.

"Newsworld" Business Reporter Jeannie Lee --- has vastly improved her hairstyle in recent years; all right, what the hell, Hot.

Aging Fashion Vulture Jeanne Bekker --- Not in a million friggin' years!!

Liberal Politico and Burning-Cross Fantasist Hedy Fry --- Not.

Pamela Anderson --- in her day, our Pammy was pure pulchritudinous physical perfection. Plus—and, as Dave Barry would say, I am not making this up—she was actually Canada's Centennial Baby (i.e., the first kid born on July 1, 1967, across the length and breadth of the entire country), which has to count for something. Getting a little long in the tooth, but still Hot!

Moody Goth Girl, always dressed in Black, into Death and Vampires and Stuff --- Not.

Golden Shiksa --- Oy vey, so Hot, you little pisher!

NDP First Lady Olivia Chow --- Hot!

Crack 'ho'... er, I Mean Sex-trade Worker with Substance-abuse Issues --- Not!

Anne of Green Gables --- Hot.

Question is Moot --- doctor has you on Paxil, or one of the other libido-butchering anti-depressants, so you couldn't get it up with a splint anyways . . . .

Winner/Loser:

Lost Castaway Evangeline Lilly --- what a sweetheart, eh?; Uber-Hotter'n hell!

Sheila Copps --- as a black hole does in space, Sheila devours the very concept of Hotness, sucks energy and light from all matter in her vicinity; Uber-Not!

(Definitely Not) Jane Taber's Hot and Not: Semi-Obligatory, Equally Offensive, Reverse-Sexist-Pig Look at Canadian Men

<u>Omar Khadr</u> --- still holding out for those 72 virgins; Not.

<u>John Baird</u> --- approaches an odd sort of Hotness when he's in full bellow at Liberals in the House of Commons; still, there's something a little "different" about him, can't quite put your finger on it; Not.

<u>Don Cherry</u> --- "every girl crazy 'bout a sharp-dressed man;" Blazing Hot, of course.

<u>Peter MacKay</u> --- all right, that standing-in-the-potato-patch-with-Rover thing was hysterical ... still, he looked so forlorn and sincere ... sigh! And have you ever seen the way he fills out those rugby shorts? Hot.

<u>Joe Clark</u> --- male equivalent of the dreaded Sheila Copps, only dumber and with a much larger lifetime legacy of misjudgment and failure; Not.

<u>David Suzuki</u> --- insufferable one-note-Nelly (yeah, we get it already, humans are destroying the goddamned environment); Not.

<u>Ed Broadbent</u> --- kindly, avuncular, principled, sincere; Not.

<u>Michael Ignatieff</u> --- so humourless and condescending, yet at the same time irritable and pretentious. Reminds you of that Poli Sci prof you had a crush on back in first-year university, who "accidentally" brushed against your left breast for a heart-stopping second too long at the end-of-term mixer; Hot! (Bonus points if he ever sees fit to trim those Cossack eyebrows.)

<u>Don Newman</u> --- on today's Braaaadcast ... Not!

<u>Ralph Benmergui</u> --- who?

<u>Lloyd Robertson</u> --- withered, desiccated old mummy; Not!

<u>Willie Pickton</u> --- you son of a bitch! That really <u>isn't</u> funny!

<u>Rick Mercer</u> --- you're a little disappointed with those "one ton challenge" sell-out commercials from a few years back, plus his increasing comfort level with the powerful (especially John Baird ... not that there's anything wrong with that); still, he'll always have a Hot place in your heart.

<u>Ian Hanomansing</u> --- oh, yeah, so Hot!

<u>Geddy Lee of *Rush*</u> --- oh, lord, so Not!

<u>Jeffery Simpson's Uncle Fred from Saltspring Island</u> --- would be sexier than his bloodless tool of a nephew if he existed as more than a lazy literary device; as it is, Not.

<u>Jim Carrey</u> --- split decision ... Hot when he sticks to making us laugh (i.e., literally talking out of his ass at awards ceremonies ... you don't run into high-brow humour like that so often these days), but Not when he's acting in a "serious" role.

<u>Alex Trebek</u> --- has all the answers on a sheet of paper right in front of him, but insists on being snotty enough to *Jeopardy* contestants who guess

wrong that he makes Ignatieff look humble. ("Etruscans? Hmphh ... oh, no, Monica, it was the Carthaginians ... Carthaginians ... Bob, you make the next selection."); Not (unless he grows back the 'stache, maybe ...).

Stockwell Day --- was Not Hot back in the callow wetsuit days of yore ... now has an endearing air of sadness about him, along with the quiet strength that only years of disappointment and adversity can impart; dumb as a bag of hammers, but Hot.

Ed the Sock --- women love Bad Boys; Hot.

Demented Fiddler Ashley MacIsaac --- like I said, women love Bad Boys ... but, since he's aggressively uninterested in women, we'll have to say Not.

Right-wing Gadfly and Recovering Stock-aholic Ezra Levant --- Not.

Self-styled Visionary and Newly Minted "Zoomer" Moses Znaimer --- Not.

Jean Charest --- would be a little bit Hot, maybe, except his resemblance to Ronald MacDonald makes you feel guilty about Happy Meal you scarfed down last week; Not.

Justin Trudeau --- pretty enough, until he opens his mouth and lets the most shamelessly vapid of platitudes (even by Liberal standards) seep forth; Not.

Ben Mulroney --- Brian's biggest mistake and deepest regret, next to which Meech Lake and those envelopes of German arms-dealer cash pale in comparison; Not.

Karlheinz Schreiber --- surprisingly H ... nah, I'm just yanking your chain; Not.

Tom Green --- massive, massive jerk, and missing a testicle; Not!

Michael J. Fox --- gonna sound heartless, but, sorry, Not anymore.

Tony Clement --- makes Bill Gates look like Fabio; Not.

Howie Mandel --- never found him remotely entertaining, or sexy; Not.

John Candy --- very entertaining, but never found him remotely sexy; Not.

William Shatner --- maybe if you were really high and he started singing his over-the-top camp-version of "Rocket Man" or "Lucy in the Sky with Diamonds;" otherwise Not.

David Frum --- integral part of the Axis of Not!

Jian Ghomeshi --- Moxy Fru-Not!

Rugged, Porn-star-mustachioed, Salt-of-the-Earth Maritime Fisherman ... er, I Mean "Fisher" --- makes a good living, and smells like love; Hot.

"Metrosexual" --- why don't you get your unnaturally soft hands off my moisturizer and mince on back to the "Lifestyle" section of the Saturday *Globe and Mail*, circa 2006, where you belong; Not!

Sidney Crosby --- Hot.

Recently Retired General Rick Hillier --- Hot.

Farley Mowat --- love the kilt, but gotta say Not.

Mr. Magoo-like Broadcasting Icon Craig Oliver --- Not.

<u>Punk-ass Wannabe Hip-hop Gangsta Hard Case, With All the Laboured,</u> <u>"Ghetto" Mannerisms and Trying-too-hard, Slightly Outdated Slang</u> --- get your shizzle to the nizzle, homey, and heed the 411; Not.

<u>Any Guy from an "Axe Body Spray" Commercial</u> --- oooo, I don't know what it is, just can't control myself; Not!

Winner and Loser:

<u>That delightful Seamus O'Regan from *Canada AM*</u> --- Uber-Hot.

<u>Mike Bullard</u> --- tempting to call him "Canada's answer to Chevy Chase," except that Chevy has actually worked in the past decade ... in reality, he's the entertainment world's fatter, more thoroughly defeated and less amusing answer to Joe Clark; Uber-Not.

Heritage Minute: Land O' Opportunity

HRDC office, September, 1995, Kitchener, Ontario:

Achmed: I don't understand what is the problem…I send out 500 CVs in last two months, and get no interviews, not one!

Employment Counselor: I appreciate your frustration, Mr. Hussein, but you know finding your first job in Canada will take patience. Have you thought any more about Blue Line?

Achmed: But I don't have taxi licence… my training is as electrical engineer.

Employment Counselor: Well, like we've discussed, most professional jobs require that you have valid work experience…

Achmed: … I work for 12 years in such field…!

Employment Counselor: … in Canada.

Achmed: How I can get experience in Canada if Canadian company won't hire me?

Employment Counselor: It's going to take some time…

Achmed: I have to get income soon, our savings is running out!

Employment Counselor: There is a driving school in Waterloo I could refer you to…it's a three-week course to get your taxi licence, then you can work part time, nights and weekends…there'll be plenty of free time to keep looking for engineering employment…

Achmed (resignedly): All right, Mr. Bertrand, as long as it's temporary…

Indian Smoke-shops

✦

"You've Come a Long Way, Baby!"

Compassionate Canadians of the Goodthinking persuasion generally concur that: a) North America was shamefully and treacherously stolen from its rightful aboriginal owners (the visible minority formerly known as "Indians") in the past, and; b) this greed-filled, deceitful, near-genocidal history, coupled with a profoundly racist and unequal socio/economic structure that continues to the present day, has left natives in a wretched, marginalized state that is "our fault," and must be atoned for (with "our mealy-mouthed apologies," as well as "our tax dollars").

Now, let me state right here that I believe "a" to be substantially true. The historical reality of the matter was no doubt more complicated and perhaps less "black and white" than many liberals will concede, and the reality itself (the bald-faced seizure of other people's land) is scarcely unique in the annals of human behavior. Still, the fact remains that (some of) our ancestors did invade and occupy this portion of the continent and, by the enlightened standards of today, that was clearly wrong.

I'm a little less convinced by proposition "b," however, or by its apparent public-policy implications … that is, that Canada should keep throwing "reparation" money at native social problems in the blind hope that this approach will miraculously alleviate them this time, when it plainly hasn't for the past 40, 50 years or so.

I'd be even less keen on the idea if I were one of the many millions of New Canadians (the visible minorities formerly known as "immigrants") now helping to pay the freight. In fact, I'd probably be feeling more than a little cheesed-off with the constant dentist-drill whine of unsatisfiable native outrage to which they, and we, are subjected, not to mention all the insufferably self-righteous guilt-mongering and cry-baby mewling for more billions of government (i.e., tax-payer) dollars to waste.

Likewise, I'd probably be starting to perceive natives, or at least their leadership caste of professional malcontents, as a selfish, aggressive and hostile bunch, spoiled rotten by decades of official "appeasement." And I'd be getting pretty sick of the various Oka/Ipperwash/Caledonia-style "occupations" that flare up regularly … you know, where the Great Turtle comes to some chief's step-cousin in a dream and reminds him that there's a sacred burial ground on a nearby parcel of land, and then suggests that 112 Mohawk Warriors should maybe spend the next year or two camped on it, burning tires and blocking traffic.

Still, while I can kinda understand how this state of affairs might be breeding a bit of resentment out there, our chattering-class "betters" appear fixated on the current model of dealing with natives, and tend to reject alternative suggestions as "racist." So, about all that the rest of us can do is sit back and try to find whatever silver lining of amusement there may be in the whole messy picture.

For me, this small ray of sunshine occurs whenever native people use their special, race-based legal status and effective semi-autonomy as "First Nations" to undercut other worthy causes that Do-Gooders hold dear. Hence the smoke-shops in this section's title: if there's anything that progressive types love more than abasing themselves before an oppressed minority, it's imposing healthful behaviour on the rest of society "for its own good."

In other words, the kind of middle-class cappuccino-slurpers who hang a friggin' "DreamCatcher" from the rear-view mirror of their Toyota Prius to demonstrate "respect for native spirituality"—that is to say, the kind of people who call Canada "our home <u>on</u> native land," and then look up at you with a sanctimonious little smirk, as if what they've said is in some way original or insightful—also tend to favour ruinous cigarette taxes and punitive smoking restrictions (or, if you prefer, Paternalistic Health Fascism).

So the sight of Indian free-marketeers happily purveying smuggled smokes to an entire multi-racial rainbow coalition of their desperately tobacco-addicted fellow citizens fills me with a disturbing amount of glee (and I gave the filthy habit up back in 1998 … pretty sure I'd be angling for a kindly native couple to adopt me if I were still in thrall to Mistress Nicotine).

This undercutting of the whole "we-know-best" mindset is even more delicious in the case of Indian-run gambling establishments that choose to flout indoor smoking bans. I mean, these casinos and bingo halls and the like are so full of second-hand smoke that they make a windless August afternoon in Los Angeles seem like the aromatherapy room in a Yorkville day-spa.

But—despite the presence of a scientifically proven health hazard so noxious and toxic that even reading about it will give you immediate, incurable emphysema—the nation's substantial agglomeration of busy-body wannabe social engineers is unable to interfere; aboriginal rights completely trump their compulsion to mandate healthy surroundings for all, whether we want 'em or not.

And that's not even the best example … if you wanna burst a New-Agey type's hitherto-undiagnosed brain aneurysm, try pitting some gentle native stewards of Mother Gaia against the holy tenets of Environmentalism. For example, I recall one time back in 1999 when the Makah tribe down in Washington state decided to reassert its traditional sovereignty and heritage by—get this—paddling out and harpooning a whale!

I was living in Vancouver at the time, and vividly remember how troubling this was for many of my tree-hugging acquaintances … their reaction reminded me for all the world of the original *Star Trek*, when Mr. Spock would destroy a malevolent, out-of-control super-computer by giving it two mutually contradictory propositions to think about, so that it starts to overheat and emit clouds of smoke, then bursts into flames and self-destructs …"Indigenous people are our moral betters … But whales are beautiful, highly intelligent beings with their own right to live peacefully in harmony with Nature … Illogical, Circuit Overload, BZZZZTTTT!!"

It's the same dynamic when Inuit fur-trappers tell Greenpeace to go pound sand, or treaty rights to a "modest food-fishery for personal use" turn into daily tractor-trailer loads of salmon heading down to the States, or a bunch of eagles get slaughtered so that their tail feathers can be used in some dubious, newly revived/invented religious ceremony … Hilarious!

None of which should be taken as suggesting that our fellow citizens of the indigenous persuasion are any worse than the rest of us scumbags. But the fact that they're just as greedy, stupid and short-sighted as anyone else in this country kinda restores a fella's faith in human nature, and is fast becoming one of the biggest reasons that I enjoy being Canadian.

Test Your Knowledge: First Nations!!!

Canada's aboriginal peoples constitute a vital, but frequently misunderstood, piece of our national cultural mosaic. This quiz will help readers to measure their own level of awareness about native issues; please bear in mind that there is only <u>one</u> correct response to each question.

1. Our country spends tens of billions of dollars every year on its First Nations. This volume of expenditure can best be described as:

   a) high, but fair (it's a necessary form of redress for past injustice and present inequities).

   b) throwing good money after bad (we've poured untold billions down this public-policy rat-hole over the past 40 years, to no apparent avail).

c) a racket (enriches a corrupt native elite, while perpetuating a bloated, self-interested bureaucracy and parasitical "aboriginal industry").

d) counterproductive (subsidizing sloth, ignorance and dysfunction pretty much guarantees that you'll get more of it).

e) grossly inadequate (public spending needs to be radically increased to address shameful, Third World conditions that besmirch Canada's international reputation. Besides which, we stole their country, man!)

f) typically, tragically, quintessentially Canadian (well meaning as all get out, but entirely disproportionate to the amount of good that's being accomplished).

2. In my opinion, aboriginal people are:

a) not making much of a positive contribution.

b) helpless, hapless, noble victims.

c) an ungrateful drain on productive citizens.

d) dignified survivors of discrimination, structural inequality, residential schools, etc.

e) slowly regaining their pride and sense of purpose after a very difficult past.

f) troubled, but entitled to whatever slack we can cut 'em.

g) lazy, drunken, solvent-huffing deadbeats.

h) sniveling sucky-babies.

i) far better than that "cancer of history," the white race.

j) individuals about whom over-generalizations are distressingly rife.

3. On watching indigenous people perform one of their sacred rituals, I am filled with:

a) a profound respect for native spirituality.

b) the same contempt I would feel for any other public example of childish superstition.

c) amusement at the pious solemnity and exaggerated deference of middle-class Caucasian onlookers.

d) deep desire for a real culture of my own, instead of the sterile, unsatisfying, Wonder-bread-strip-mall purgatory in which I was raised.

e) anger that Christian rituals are everywhere derided and disparaged, while this kind of pagan heathenism is not only tolerated but officially encouraged.

f) interest and curiosity.

g) boredom and incomprehension.

4. Any solution to the serious social problems faced by Canada's native population has to be based upon:

a) true assimilation/integration into society.

b) complete autonomy and self-rule for each and every First Nation.

c) more sensitivity and understanding.

d) good old-fashioned genocide ("cultural genocide," whatever the hell that is, is clearly taking too long).

e) their using a little elbow grease, showing some moxie, pulling themselves up by their own bootstraps (or moccasin flaps, or whatever), etc.

f) immediate capitulation on all outstanding land claims, thereby giving aboriginals a solid economic base on which to build.

g) the settler races either returning to whatever continents they came from, or agreeing to stay on provisionally as "tenants" of Turtle Island.

h) smallpox-infected blankets, free firewater.

i) strict separation from mainstream society … aboriginals should be allowed to return to living in harmony with nature, away from contamination of the modern world.

j) strict separation from mainstream society … aboriginals should be forced to return to living at the mercy of nature, away from blessings of the modern world.

k) repatriating the whole works of 'em back across the Bering Strait to Asia.

l) bringing in the US cavalry to kick their asses.

m) requiring all members of the Iroquois confederacy to apologize and atone for the historical enslavement/slaughter of their neighbours, such as the Huron, Erie and Neutral tribes.

n) Paul Martin's crowning achievement, the Kelowna Accord.

o) something different from the strategies hitherto employed.

Answers: 1) f 2) j 3) c 4) o.

Painfully Earnest, Do-Goodish Boy-Scoutism

✦

"Won't Somebody PLEEAASE Think of the Children?"

It's easy to mock the desperate, almost neurotic need many Canadians seem to have to remake this country (and the whole friggin' planet, if its largely disinterested denizens would pay any attention) into a Better, Fairer, More Compassionate Place, chock-full of Caring, Sharing and State-Funded Hugs for the Underprivileged.

It's even easier to make fun when the entire record of human history demonstrates with depressing regularity that Really Good Intentions often lead to Unexpectedly Lousy Consequences (see earlier section on Trudeau … also consult available reference works on communism and, to varying degrees, every other ideology and religion that has ever existed).

But, after a certain point, ridiculing people who so sincerely ache to Do Nice Things for the poor, afflicted, benighted, malodorous masses ceases to be any fun … it's sorta like kicking a goofy puppy that got really excited while it was fetching your slipper and accidentally widdled on the living-room carpet.

And, after your foot connects with its posterior, it cringes and stares up at you with big, wounded eyes, questioning: "Why? What did I do? I thought I was <u>helping</u>!" And you wind up just patting it on the head and spritzing the wet spot with some Spray N' Wash to try and get rid of the pee-stank.

So, no matter how irritating their high-pitched yelping and whining may sometimes be, no matter how much of a stain they may sometimes leave on the nation's metaphorical carpet, I try not to be too hard on the Sincerely Well-Meaning; in many ways they are far "nicer" people than those of us with a more realistic take on the world, and, in a complicated way, they probably contribute to some of the things that make Canada a decent place to live.

For example, I believe our country owes much of its fabled reputation for being "nice" and "polite" (or, as some would have it, "bland" and "boring") to this do-goody underpinning. Now, as with Canada's exuberant abundance of "space," any alleged "politeness" may only become apparent when you travel elsewhere; still, as browned off as you may sometimes get with certain of your fellow Canucks, I'll willing to bet that most friggin' foreigners will strike you as ruder, pushier and more in-your-face abrasive by far (and *oui*, France, you are *tete* of the class once again. Well done!)

Which is not to imply that we Canadians are all Emily-Post-studying, pinkie-in-the-air quaffers of milk-tea and nibblers of watercress sandwiches with the crusts cut off. But any kind of foreign travel will soon show you that the humble, underrated practice of actually lining up for stuff and waiting your goddamn turn is a rare and precious virtue in this world.

Sure, I suppose it is kind of pathetic when you step on a Canadian's foot and he conforms to hoary cliché by saying "Sorry." Still, all things considered, it's better to have that basic bedrock layer of civility than it is to have the guy curse your whore-mother for spawning such a clumsy imbecile, and then shove a sharpened screwdriver into your gut.

When it comes right down to it, I <u>like</u> living in a country where strangers still have enough goodwill to stop and help push your hopelessly stuck car out of a snowdrift. Similarly, I <u>like</u> the fact that Canadian bus passengers will usually move their ungainly mukluked feet a token little amount out of the way to let me get by when I'm edging down the aisle.

And I <u>really</u> like it when two of us are walking towards each other on a narrow path through the snow, and we both step off to opposite sides and flounder along for a few feet 'til we pass rather than seem like a trail-hog … I mean, it's moronic, but it shows a basic respect and consideration, a <u>recognition that the other person exists, and has value,</u> that ought not to be underestimated.

So, when it comes right down to it, and despite its frequently annoying manifestations, I would have to say that politeness is another good reason to enjoy being Canadian. (If that's all right with you guys….)

Heritage Minute: After You, Eh!

Monday morning, residential neighborhood of Ottawa, Ontario, January, 2008:

"Tabernouche!" muttered Jacques, as the wind picked up and the snow came at him almost horizontally along Bank Street. A pick-up truck slid past, barely under control, and splattered the sidewalk with slush; then someone spied the bus and a hopeful murmur rippled through the little knot of stamping, shivering commuters.

Jacques and the others watched as the Number 1 fishtailed towards their stop, ground to a reluctant halt and swung open its door. As always, the men held back until each female in the group had stepped aboard, and then followed; it'd be standing room only for them to downtown, as usual, but at least they'd be warm.

Pogey

✦

"Somethin' for Nothin'? Where Do I Sign Up?"

Growing up in Cape Breton gives a fella a bit of a skewed perspective on Canada's Unemployment (sorry, I mean "Employment") Insurance system.

I've seen it help folks who truly need it. But I've also watched scores of people abuse the plan, mercilessly, year after year. And I'm pretty sure that the perverse disincentives built into its very structure have acted to immobilize Maritime workers and inhibit local development.

One thing I am sure of, though, is that pogey isn't the same as welfare.

See, I was on the dole one time, back in the evil, recessionary summer of 1992, when the Canadian economy was in its most decrepit and enfeebled state in many a year.

As luck would have it, I had just graduated from university, and was busy finding out how useful my Very Impressive Degree was in the Real World. ("C'mon, we can't give this menial, ill-paid, entry-level job to you, you've got no experience.")

So, following the ancient migratory patterns of my Atlantic Canadian forebears, I eventually wound up moving to Toronto, renting a small, cockroach-ridden room above a place called Olga's Tavern (exactly as classy as it sounds), and signing up for "social assistance."

As I recall, about 90 percent of my fellow tenants at Olga's were older, single guys who had been unemployed for years, and seemed to be of little use to themselves or anyone else. Indeed, most of them went on great, reeking binges for days at a time when the welfare cheques came in, and, when sober, were fully as indolent as the stereotypes would have it. (Younger fellows, as is only appropriate, had a little more initiative; they were out there every day, pulling petty cons, panhandling, stealing, peddling a bit of crack, and so on.)

Thing was, though, I understood their behaviour more and more as the summer wore on. 'Cause I found myself getting drunk, too, and smoking whatever dope I could get my hands on, whenever I had the money (though I could ill afford it, and was often literally penniless by the end of the month as a direct result).

This was not because of "peer pressure," or anything like that, either. It was a reaction—a really stupid reaction—to the frustration of beating my head against a wall of job market rejection; to the humiliation of being unneeded, superfluous, a failure; to the boredom, loneliness and worry inherent in being very poor. (Drugs are not the answer, they tell kids, but the fact is that drugs—booze of course pre-eminent among them—most assuredly are the answer when the question is: "How do I blot this miserable, intolerable crap from my mind for a few hours?")

And I was a reasonably bright, able-bodied young man—for your run-of-the-mill Olga's-dweller, prospects were far grimmer. Forty, fifty, sixty years old, uneducated, unhealthy, uncouth, unskilled—they had nothing going for them, and knew it.

Yeah, if life can be likened to a card game, these fellas had usually been dealt some pretty lousy hands to begin with—bad childhoods, poor schools, underlying pre-dispositions to mental illness and substance abuse, the simple, inborn, crippling fact of unintelligence, etc. Expecting them to compete on an equal footing in the labour market was like expecting a 98-pound weakling to square off against a Sumo wrestler, or a retarded person to master calculus and discourse learnedly on Spinoza.

◆   ◆   ◆

I'm a lot better off, in every way, these days. But I try to keep that experience in mind whenever I stroll downtown, and encounter the whole spare-change-begging, dumpster-scavenging, sqeegee-wielding, cooking-sherry-guzzling, narcotic-injecting gamut of riffraff a Canadian city has to offer.

These people are, objectively speaking, losers. But I have no idea what lies underneath the scumbag exteriors, in their hearts and minds, or what circumstances landed them where they are. Nor do I begrudge the poor bastards whatever meager crumbs they manage to shake off the welfare table; indeed, for all the system's manifest imperfections, for all that people may fall through the cracks, or cheat and take shameless advantage, the fact that our society does try (however imperfectly) to provide something to its least fortunate and most screwed-up members is one of the things I cherish about being Canadian.

Test your Knowledge: Mental Health

While social class has a undeniable effect on our state of mind, individual thought- and behavior patterns ultimately play the determining role in each Canadian's mental health. This quiz is designed to help you identify areas of your own "psychic map" that may be holding you back; to this end, please choose the <u>one</u> response to each question that most accurately reflects your own attitude, experience or reaction.

1. When faced with serious frustration or setbacks in life, I tend to:

    a) kill a man just to watch him die.
    b) lash out blindly at weaker loved ones, family members.
    c) sacrifice neighbourhood pets to Satan.
    d) talk it out with my partner or a trusted friend, clergyperson, etc.
    e) pay a trans-gendered dominatrix to flog me with barbed wire.
    f) fantasize about wreaking bloody vengeance on the other postal workers.
    g) sell Grandma's TV, wedding band, walker, etc., go on three-day crack cocaine binge.
    h) carve obscenities into my flesh with a razor blade.

2. Which historical figure would you most like to have been?

    a) Napoleon b) Eva Braun c) Judas Iscariot d) Liberace e) Francisco Franco f) Janis Joplin g) Pol Pot h) J. Edgar Hoover i) Colonel Sanders j) Vlad the Impaler k) Barney Rubble **l) Gandhi**.

3. Which description best fits your core self-concept? I am a:

    a) good person, basically, though lord knows I have my share of faults.
    b) major disappointment, considering my early potential.
    c) ticking time bomb.
    d) Purifying Angel of Death.
    e) worthless parasite.
    f) flabby, smelly, pasty-white computer dork.
    g) twisted, evil genius.

4. Which animal best symbolizes your inner self?

a) jackass b) sloth c) pig d) bitch e) maggot f) duck-billed platypus g) vulture h) toad i) blowfish j) jackal k) lemming l) worm m) cockroach n) leech o) rat p) louse q) **fox** r) weasel.

5. In a similar vein, with which fictional or famous animal do you most closely identify?

a) drummer "Animal" from the *Muppet Show*.
b) Goofy.
c) Old Yeller.
d) Mrs. O'Leary's cow.
e) Foghorn Leghorn.
f) Flipper.
g) Dino Flintstone.
h) sociopathic mouse "Itchy" from *The Simpsons*.
i) cheese-eating surrender monkey.
j) Wile E. Coyote
k) Snuffle-upagus.

6. What do you see when you turn off the lights?

a) I can't tell you, but it sure feels like mine.
b) an endless, obsessive playback-loop of past humiliations and failures.
c) streetlight glinting off that pile of gin bottles in the corner.
d) sheep, occasionally in lingerie.
e) nothing, but I can hear Mom and my new "uncle" through the wall.
f) weird, swirling, geometric flashbacks from my last LSD trip.
g) visions of sugarplums dancing in my head, interspersed with fleeting images of Stephen Harper's stomach jiggling like a bowlful of jelly.

7. As I rise to greet each new morning, I ordinarily feel:

a) vapid b) either despairing or megalomaniacal, depending on the day c) trapped **d) eager to continue my voyage of spiritual and emotional growth** e) like my "Inner Child" just wet the bed again f) hung-over g) patricidal h) myself all over, for a few minutes.

8. Parental relationships during one's formative years have a profound influence on our mental health status as adults. Complete this statement: "Looking back on my childhood, I now see that my father was a ... ."

    a) deeply conflicted "closet queen" **b) firm but fair role-model** c) vindictive petty tyrant d) pathetic white-bread suburban drone e) habitual felon f) hairy, illiterate baboon g) near-stranger who alternated frenetic, guilt-induced attempts to buy my love with long stretches of complete absence.

9. "Looking back on my childhood, I now see that my mother was a ... ."

    a) good-natured doormat b) shrill, demanding harpy c) driven, pathologically ambitious career woman who was never really there for any of us d) sloppy, emotionally abusive drunk e) smothering, guilt-tripping meddler f) passive-aggressive ball of neuroses g) good friend to sailors **h) person I never truly appreciated at the time**.

Answers: 1) d 2) l 3) a 4) q 5) f 6) a 7) d 8) b 9) h.

Affinity Programs

♦

"'Somethin' for Nothin'? Where Do I Sign Up?'
Redux"

Has there existed a Canadian heart so cold that it failed to flutter a bit at the prospect of joining this nation's exclusive "Club Zed?" (Not for us the tinsel and temptations of yon Great Satan's morbidly obese, neo-imperialistic and celebrity gossip-obsessed "Club Zee"…) And did true patriot hearts not bleed, ever so briefly, on the dark day that this properly-pronounced-26th-letter Club was puréed into the generic corporate mush of something called the "HBC Rewards program?"

Still, in the fullness of time, our ever-resilient country managed to dust itself off, gird its collective loins and re-focus on what's important—no matter what some head-office gearbox decides to call the damn thing, you can still get free stuff if ya collect enough of their silly-ass points.

For Canadians are above all a practical people, much-given to the idea of receiving some "incentive" for buying things that we were going to purchase anyway. Thus, for example, the well-known national fondness for "Air Miles." (This devotion is, of course, especially pronounced among boozehounds, given that these thingies can be "earned" at liquor stores in most provinces.

Although I've never been entirely clear on why—I mean, there <u>are</u> no private-sector competitors to the LCBO in Ontario, for example, so thirsty lushes would scarcely seem to need a loyalty-program bribe to patronize the place. Seriously, has a single solitary soul in Canadian history ever purchased <u>more</u> spirituous beverages than otherwise intended in order to <u>get a few extra "Air Miles</u>?" And would it be a particularly good thing if someone <u>had</u>?)

Similarly, many of us seem to derive great satisfaction from collecting "Aeroplan" points (redeemable for low- and shoulder-season midweek red-eye travel, every third leap year—still, it's so gratifying to wring <u>something</u> out of those Air-oflot Canada SOBs that we enjoy every second of the free flight, including the edited-to-tatters-family-movie-starring-a-sadly-diminished-Eddie-Murphy and the 90-minute de-icing delay).

And I dunno about you, but I've become a <u>big</u>, big fan of the Shoppers Drug Mart Optimum card. In fact—being a really, really, really cheap prick—I save every conceivable health-related purchase until one of those weekends when they have a "20 times the regular Optimum points on total bills of $50.00 or more" extravaganza. Coupla scores like that add up, boy—next time you saunter in, you're looking at a cool $50 or $75.00 worth of *gratis* goodies.

◆   ◆   ◆

Much as we may enjoy and profit from them, though, these programs are mere trifles compared to the 800-pound-gorilla-riding-sidesaddle-on-the-elephant-in-the-room of domestic affinity marketing: Canadian Tire money.

Is there a fictional figure more beloved in this country than the Canadian Tire bills' happily mustachioed, twinkly-eyed, rakish-tam-o-shanter-sportin' icon, Sandy McTire? Hell, is there a <u>real</u> figure in this country, in the fields of politics, business, entertainment, or even sports, whose visage is more likely than Mr. McTire's to provoke a delighted grin of recognition from your average Canuck?

Oh, we love our Canadian Tire moolah, we do. Odds are you've got a few bucks worth squirreled away in the back of a drawer at this very moment (hey, since the stock market kamikaze-ed into a subprime-mortgaged fireworks factory in Fall '08, that little stash may well be the most valuable remaining component of your investment portfolio).

And, oddly enough, our attachment to the funny money is entirely independent of any feelings we may have for Canadian Tire itself ... I mean, I've got nothing against the company at all, but it's literally been years since I've set foot in one of their stores.

Still, I hold on to my little hoard, just like you. And you know why? 'Cause it <u>feels</u> real: according to (the apparently indispensable) Wikipedia, Canadian Tire bills "have the same paper content and spot marks as actual legal tender," and incorporate the latest anti-counterfeiting technology (including "a latent image of a maple leaf to the right side of Sandy McTire's left ear" ... go on, check; I'll wait.)

Yup, it's just that kind of quality and attention to detail (not to mention the prospect of one day redeeming the stuff for a discount on some necessary good or service) that Canucks truly appreciate. Which is why this affinity program, in particular, occupies an honoured place in the pantheon of reasons to enjoy being Canadian.

Heritage Minute: The Death Camp of Tolerance

West End of Vancouver, British Columbia, May, 2008:

Adam and Steve strolled down Davie Street in their finest leather jockstraps, holding hands and almost giddy with new love. Each time they had to wait at a crosswalk, one of them would press in against the other and kiss him, with a tenderness and passion that never failed to elicit warm smiles from all who witnessed it.

Within a few minutes, they reached Denman Street, and turned left onto the beach. Small groups of people, young and old, were already gathered there, chatting in mellow tones, the odour of their BC Bud pungent against the low-tide smell of the Pacific.

Steve found an unoccupied log a little ways up the sand and sat down to admire the sunset; Adam remained standing and lit a "Rothman's." At this, a jogger instantly stopped, sniffed the air and scowled; from 30 feet away, Adam could just make out the logo on her T-shirt: "Celebrate Diversity: Practice Random Acts of Tolerance."

"Please," she hissed. "No smoking!"

Warm, Furry Beavers

✦

"No, This Isn't One of Them Double-Entendres ... I Really Do Mean The Fur-bearing Mammal"

○ ○

"The beaver, a four-footed animal that lives in pools, knows that he is hunted for his testicles, which are used to cure ailments. When pursued, the beaver runs for some distance, but when he sees that he cannot escape, he will bite off his own testicles and throw them to the hunter, and thus escape death."

Pliny the Elder, 1ˢᵗ Century AD

Typical, ain't it? Most countries associate themselves with <u>cool</u> critters—the Russian bear, Chinese dragon, Thai elephant, British bulldog, American eagle, French *Pepé Le Pew*.

Not Canada, though: when asked to choose from a veritable smorgasbord of potential emblematic animals—your majestic moose, fierce cougar, stout-hearted musk-ox, tasty caribou, dangerously-unbalanced loon, mutant-superhero Wolverine, Al-Gore-claims-it's-endangered-by-global-warming-though-I-see-very-little-hard-evidence polar bear—we opt for a funky-smelling, buck-toothed rodent of such legendary moral cowardice that it apparently <u>chomps off its own family jewels</u> when under threat.

The perfect Canadian symbol, eh ...?

•   •   •

Well, it is and it ain't.

I mean, sure, auto-testicle-munchin' makes a heck of a story (even by Pliny-the-Elder standards) ... but c'mon, there's no life-form in the known universe <u>that's gonna chew through its own ball-sack</u>, no matter what the circumstances (let alone scamper away to safety afterwards)!

Nope, poor old Mr. Beaver remains what he's always been—a small, homely, consistently underrated, endearingly unflashy figure, noted for his diligence, pluck and quiet perseverance (not to mention his resolutely ungnawed gonads).

Or in other words, the perfect national symbol—and as such, yet another reason to enjoy being Canadian.

Test your Knowledge: Canadian Men!!!

Although Canadian men and women share a roughly equivalent degree of interest in dam-building mammals, they differ in many other key respects. This quiz is designed to aid both sexes, by deepening women's understanding of the typical male psyche, and assisting men in the difficult quest for self-knowledge. To these ends, please choose <u>one</u> response to each of the following questions.

1. When together in a group, men often talk about:

    a) their latest bout of impotence.
    b) the cutesy "baby talk" language they use in private moments with the wife/girlfriend.
    c) phallocentrism.
    d) new evidence of the "undeclared war against women" now raging in popular culture.
    e) favourite *Golden Girls* episodes.
    f) the short stories of Joyce Carol Oates.
    g) high-spirited and/or drunken escapades from their youth.
    h) how they wish society would permit them to cry and show vulnerability.

2. Typical, much-loved male pastimes include:

    a) surreptitiously comparing "sizes" in public restrooms.
    b) hosting Tupperware parties.
    c) laughing boorishly at "snuff" films.
    d) maliciously holding doors for able-bodied females in order to demean them.
    e) pulling out scalp hair and gluing it to their backs, knuckles, beer bellies, etc.
    f) taking long, sensuous bubble baths.

g) paying child support.

h) bombing upstart Third World nations back into the Stone Age.

i) trying to impress each other.

3. Men also love to:

a) help pick out patterns or material.

b) buy tampons for their ailing or busy partners.

c) be reminded of that old cliché about how "all men hate to ask for directions" when <u>we're not lost, dammit</u>.

d) pick up the check.

e) keep track of trivial pseudo-anniversaries, like the date of your first meeting, first kiss, first child's birth, first marriage-counseling appointment, etc.

f) be personally blamed for all past and present injustices against women (people of colour, gays, handicapped spotted owls, etc.) from the very dawn of time.

g) complain about women.

4. The female physical features found most attractive by men are:

a) "meth mouth."

b) big warts with long, black hair curling out of 'em.

c) open sores that don't heal.

d) discoloured, furry teeth, matted hair, feral body odor.

e) bald spots and pot bellies.

f) "Property of Satan's Choice Motorcycle Club" tattoos.

g) dangerous to say for fear of being thought a sexist objectifier, although, quite honestly, soft curves and ample bosoms come into it somewhere.

5. Men are:

a) from Mars.

b) pigs.

c) immature, commitment-phobic Peter Pans.

d) all potential rapists.

e) either flaccid, simpering "New Man" sissies or unreconstructed, flatulent chauvinists.

f) mostly trying the best they can in confusing times, and getting precious little credit for it.

g) life support systems for penises (penii?).

h) diverse creatures about whom all but one of the above statements contain some grain of truth.

6. Men prefer women who are:

    a) chocolate-gorging *Oprah*-holics.
    b) ruthlessly ambitious competitors.
    c) insecure and clingy.
    d) over-disposed to talking about "the relationship" in great depth and detail.
    e) nagging ball-breakers.
    f) recent, successful participants in a precedent-setting "PMS"-based murder defence.
    g) a combination of their mother, their best buddy, and a depraved strumpet (in the appropriate situations).
    h) comically scatter-brained, in the Gracie Allen mode.
    i) inflatable.

7. One topic that "regular guys" <u>never</u> discuss is:

    a) carburetors.
    b) the Stanley Cup playoffs.
    c) Internet porn sites.
    d) Richard Simmons' *Sweatin' to the Oldies*.
    e) the new "Hooters" restaurant downtown.
    f) whether it's "cold/hot/wet enough for ya."
    g) how "they" are hangin'.
    h) mammaries.
    i) taxes.

8. Which of the following statements made by men to women is <u>never</u> a lie?

    a) I love you too.
    b) really, I had to work.
    c) no, it doesn't make you look fat.
    d) sure, I was listening.
    e) oh, yeah, I noticed your new (dress, hat, haircut, purse, life-threatening illness, etc.)
    f) I don't understand it, this never happened to me before.
    g) no, no, it's not because of you.
    h) I hate your parents.

9. Many men would welcome a "dirty weekend" with:

   a) Beyonce and any two of the *Pussycat Dolls*.
   b) spacey Icelandic chanteuse Bjork and brainwashed Scientological spouse Katie Holmes.
   c) the Olsen twins.
   d) a *Cirque du Soleil* contortionist and Jessica Alba.
   e) Madonna and Rosie O'Donnell.
   f) Roseanne Barr and Jenna Jameson.
   g) ex-*Beatle* squeezes Heather Mills and Yoko Ono.
   h) skeletal gubernatorial spouse Maria Shriver and enormous drag queen RuPaul.
   i) eternally entertaining train wrecks Courtney Love and Amy Winehouse.
   j) Squeaky Fromme and Bif Naked.
   k) any and all of the above (dude, we're guys!)

Answers:

1) g 2) i 3) g 4) g 5) h 6) g 7) d 8) h 9) k.

Hockey

✦

"Tweeeeeet!... That's You, Richard ... Two Minutes For Lookin' So Good!"

The wife, as I may have mentioned, is one of them inscrutable-foreigner types (rather than a "Real Canadian," like you and me). Nonetheless, she's lived in various parts of this country since 1998 and, as such, has become fairly well-acquainted with our national character (in particular, our apparent propensity towards leaving the bathroom in an unholy mess after we shave, as well as scattering goddamned smelly socks all over the bedroom floor. Also "forgetting birthdays" and "never taking me anywhere").

Gratifyingly enough, her perception of the Canuck character tends (with certain, previously noted exceptions) to be a positive one—thus, in her experience, Canadians as a whole really <u>are</u> as low-key, nice and polite as we constantly tell everybody that we are.

The one glaring exception, for her, is hockey. Indeed, she persists in perceiving the national pastime as an almost unbelievably thuggish species of primitive gladiatorial combat, at total odds with our otherwise peaceful self-image.

Being a "Real Canadian," I have naturally done my best to convince her that the repellent violence evident in our national pastime is part of the reason we're so famously placid in the rest of our daily lives—that all the fore-checking and board-crunching and glove-dropping and spitting-out-of-tooth-fragments-after-bench-clearing-brawling and such has a <u>cathartic</u> effect, allowing us to discharge our pent-up aggression and murderous misanthropy in a relatively safe and structured venue.

Don't know if I've convinced the Little Woman yet (although, now that you mention it, she <u>did</u> shove me into a corner and slash the hell outta my shins with a broom-handle the other day...); but, if nothing else, she now agrees that hockey is one of the things the rest of us enjoy about being Canadian.

Heritage Minute: I Like To Rock!!!

April Wine *concert, Canadian National Exhibition, Toronto, Ontario, August, 2007:*

George was killing time over by the fence, slugging back his fourth cup of lukewarm Labatts *and surveying the crowd.*
"Cripers, when'd we all turn middle-aged?" he thought to himself, with wry amusement.
A small sea of graying rockers stood between him and the stage, all blue-collar faces and unfashionable hair, faded denim and ball caps, beer bellies and blowsy women talking way too loud.

And then the band started up, and George was at one with his people, adulthood forgotten, howling like he was 14 again: "Yeahhhhhh, April Wiiiine, Yeahhhh!!!"

Canadian Arts/Literature (and Other Dangers/Annoyances)

✦

"Where's My Grant Cheque? I've Got Rich Galas To Attend, And Taxpaying Philistines At Whom To Sneer!"

If this world can be seen as a vast "Family of Nations," then Canada is surely its "Funny Uncle" … .

…Hmmm, that may have come out wrong. Just to be clear, I'm not comparing our beloved country to the moist-lipped, middle-aged-bachelor-uncle who used to try and wrestle you every weekend … I mean "funny=ha, ha," not "funny=borderline-indictable."

Anyway, the point I'm (rather tastelessly) trying to make is that Canada generates far more than its fair share of Highly Humourous People: witness Brent Butt, Ron James, the casts of *SCTV*, *Royal Canadian Air Farce*, *CODCO*, and *This Hour has 22 Minutes*, not to mention the various and sundry yuksters we've exported to the States over the years (Rich Little, Leslie Nielsen, Dan Aykroyd, Mike Myers, Jim Carrey, Norm Macdonald, Will Arnett, Russell Peters, Seth Rogen, to name but a few).

All of which kinda begs the question: why—given our proven affinity and apparent national talent for humour—must all of Canada's other creative arts-type endeavours be such a massive, monochromatic <u>drag</u>?

"CanLit," for instance, has pretty much imploded into total self-parody: how many *Fall-On-Your-Knees*-style tales of small-town despair/alcoholism/incest does it really take to drive home the message that Life Sucks and Existence is Meaningless? (I don't necessarily disagree, but why keep belabouring the point—believe me, it's all been said before.)

And Canadian cinema ("CanCin?") is, if anything, even more of a downer: all Implacably Dull, Head-Up-The-Director's-Own-Very-Pretentious-Ass

Symbolism and Unrelievedly Downbeat Studies in Whiny Angst ... watch one of these whimsy-fests straight through and you're liable to find yourself out in the garage at midnight, frantically stringing a hose from the exhaust pipe to your driver's-side window.

◆   ◆   ◆

The only real ray of sunshine gleaming through this chilly fogbank o' art is Canadian music.

Not a lot of anguish here, as a rule: just good old meat-'n'-potatoes mullet-rock, from the likes of the *Guess Who, Bachman Turner Overdrive, Trooper, Triumph,* Tom Cochrane, Kim Mitchell, Jeff Healey, the *Tragically Hip, Nickelback...*

Or, in other words, the kind of down-to-earth, crowd-pleasin' tunes that most of us (music critics excepted) enjoy about being Canadian.

Test Your Knowledge: The Creative Arts!!!

Canadian artists provide us with invaluable insights into the national soul (and, indeed, into the universal human condition). To measure your overall knowledge of and attitude towards their work, please choose <u>one</u> response to each of the following questions:

1. My most enjoyable Canadian music-related experience involved:

    a) pot.
    b) laughing my ass off at Corey Hart's pouty-faced "Never Surrender" video.
    c) laughing my ass off at Gord Downie's demented stream-of-consciousness conversation with a friggin' <u>mike stand</u> during a *Tragically Hip* concert.
    d) actually hearing Stompin' Tom Connors play "On a Sudbury Saturday Night" once, <u>in Sudbury</u>.
    e) pogo-dancing into the man who would become my husband at a *Payola$* gig.
    f) doing *Men Without Hats'* "Safety Dance" with a super-sexy Montreal chick.
    g) finally getting rid of the "hockey hair" in 1992, after realizing how much it resembled Tom Cochrane's awful, awful 'do of the time.
    h) sleeping with Leonard Cohen in the '60s.

i) guzzling two full bottles of Robitussin before a *Glass Tiger* performance and mercifully passing out for the entire thing.

j) "shivving" a rival gang member, just after *BTO* finished filming a video in the prison-yard.

k) dropping a half-tab of acid and feeling serenely self-righteous while listening to Buffy Ste. Marie.

l) finding out that my drunken heckling had inspired Valdy's "Play Me a Rock 'n' Roll Song."

m) singing along to Youtube video of a warm and sweater-y Stephen Harper belting out "With a Little Help From My Friends."

n) lighting some scented candles and listening to Sarah McLachlan in a warm bubble bath.

o) the long-gone vigour of youth.

2. Conversely, my <u>worst</u> Canadian music-related experience involved:

a) playing a *Rush* cassette backwards, only to discover the disembodied voice of Ayn Rand urging me to "love capitalism" and "embrace selfishness."

b) a Neil Young screech from the stereo that shattered every piece of glass in the house.

c) hearing some rapper say "a'xe" instead of "ask" for the 100th time.

d) hearing some rapper say "a'ight" instead of "all right" for the 500th time.

e) hearing Paul Schaffer laugh sycophantically at a lame Letterman joke for the 10,000[th] time.

f) feeling creepy all over after listening to Nick Gilder's "Hot Child in the City."

g) slam-dancing into some skinheads at a *Forgotten Rebels* show and spending the next six weeks in hospital.

h) getting pregnant in the backseat of my boyfriend's Camaro, to the strains of one of *Triumph's* many excellent power ballads.

i) getting suspended from junior high after I took *Trooper's* "Raise a Little Hell" way too seriously.

j) being the only non-stoned person ever to attend the Vancouver planetarium's *Pink Floyd* laser light show.

k) catching a regrettable glimpse of Ashley MacIsaac's weiner when he was jumping around in a kilt onstage.

l) learning the heartbreaking news that Stephen Page had left the *Bare Naked Ladies*.

m) seeing my daughter in an *Anvil* video.

n) uncontrollable projectile vomiting every time I heard the Dan Hill song "Sometimes When We Touch" on the radio in the '70s.

3. Aside from music, my favourite creative outlet involves:

   a) snowmobiling.
   b) whiffing beer bottles at stop signs.
   c) clubbing baby seals.
   d) exploiting tar sands.
   e) growing dope.
   f) designing palindromes at Mensa meetings.
   g) performing feminist interpretive dance celebrating indigenous folkways.
   h) sketching monster trucks.
   i) filming tantric-sex sessions.
   j) organizing cockfights.
   k) writing short stories about how Women's Voices Must Be Heard!
   l) suppressing 'roid rage.
   m) acting out favourite scenes from the movie *Slapshot*.
   n) something intensely personal that I'd rather not get into right now.

4. While Canadian authors have turned out some excellent, and indeed world-class, work over the decades, they have also been responsible for their share of "duds," mostly now long out-of-print. Examples of these forgotten books include:

   a) Morley Callaghan's loosely disguised *roman-a-clef* about Paris in the '20's, entitled *Hemingway Was a Fag*.
   b) Roch Carrier's subtle allegory of French-English relations, *The Hockey Cup*.
   c) Douglas Coupland's ode to the Baby Boom, *Generation Excellent*.
   d) Robertson Davies' *A High Anglican Upper Canadian Discourses on Jungian Psychology At Great Length*.
   e) Timothy Findley's magical-realist epic, *The Whores*.
   f) William Gibson's first attempt at post-modern cyber-punk, disappointingly set in Saskatoon.
   g) Margaret Laurence's raw, unflinchingly honest examination of life in a Prairie motorcycle gang, *The Stoned Angel*.
   h) Hugh MacLennan's unexpected *Calvinism Sucks*.

i) Farley Mowat's equally surprising *Wolves Suck*.

j) Mordecai Richler's *Long Live a Free Quebec!*

k) anything by any of the younger Richlers.

l) Alistair MacLeod's darkly comic *No Small Trainspotting*, about a young Cape Bretoner's descent into heroin addiction during a search for his Scottish roots in Edinburgh.

m) Yann Martel's enigmatic *The Riddle of Pie* (an East Indian boy, tiger, duck and bag of grain have to make it across the river on a raft, which, unfortunately, can only support two of them at any given time …).

n) Lucy Maude Montgomery's long-suppressed tale of yearning and forbidden passion, *Anne and her Bosom Friend*.

5. The most depressing Canadian movie of all time is:

a) *Goin' Down the Road*.

b) *Marion Bridge*.

c) *New Waterford Girl*.

d) *Margaret's Museum*.

e) *Trailer Park Boys: The Movie*.

f) *The Sweet Hereafter*.

g) *Porky's*.

h) *The Robe*.

i) *The Decline of the American Empire*.

j) *Jesus of Montreal*.

k) *A History of Violence*.

l) *Duct Tape Forever*.

m) *Thirty Two Short Films about Glenn Gould*.

n) *Passchendaele*.

o) a choppily edited porno I once caught on City TV's late-night "Baby Blue Movies."

p) a choppily edited, badly dubbed porno I once saw on the French channel's "Blue Nuit."

q) Bon Cop, Bad Cop.

Answers:

1) o 2) n 3) n 4) k 5) q.

Freedom to be an Idiot

✦

"Hey, Careful There, Dipshit!"

For a number of complex reasons (all of which are our own damned fault), Canadians have spent the last 40 years or so listening to various government Busybody-ocracies moralize and hector and "guide" their beliefs and behaviour in a "sensitive," "considerate," tooth-achingly "tolerant" direction.

Which is annoying enough. Still, prissy PC finger-wagging is one thing … as with the prattling of your well-meaning Grandma, you are free to ignore, grudgingly follow or whole-heartedly embrace this advice, as you so desire.

But when Granny's holding a gun to your head—all right, I'm getting a little carried away here (or maybe having one of those "suppressed memory" flashbacks that were all the rage there for a while)—I mean, when she has the power to fine or otherwise legally sanction you should you disregard her suggestions (entirely sensible and wholesome though they may be), it's a whole different kettle o' *poissons*.

◆   ◆   ◆

Bicycle helmets, for example, are expensive, a pain in the neck to keep track of, and ugly as gum disease. Worse, they were mandatory in Vancouver when I lived there a few years ago, and I resented the hell out of it.

I know, wheelbarrow-loads of studies have shown that helmets save lives, prevent crippling injuries, help mend the ozone layer and foster racial harmony … there was no doubt in my mind even then that they were Wonderful Things, that, dorky-looking or not, everybody <u>should</u> wear one. I just disagreed with the <u>must</u> nature of the deal, is all.

Fact is, there's a whole buncha stuff in the world that we <u>should</u> do, but on which, in the final analysis, we are all free to make up our own minds. I, for instance, <u>should</u> stop drinking to wretched, sodden, reeking excess so very, very often. I <u>should</u> quit eating Bacon Double Cheeseburgers and Spam sandwiches (at least in the same sitting). I <u>should</u> drag my sorry butt off the sofa and exercise, or take a computer course, or help the wife with dinner, or do <u>something</u> constructive, someday!

But, when last I checked, these were all still personal choices, actions that I, as a non-incarcerated citizen over the age of 21, could decide upon for myself (although, statistically, booze, cholesterol and sloth do people <u>way</u> more damage than bike accidents).

Or what about tobacco? People can still choose to smoke (even on Vancouver bicycles, as long as they're wearing a goddamn helmet), despite the actual <u>probability</u> of harming their health. We can, if so inclined, run with scissors, frolic semi-naked outside in a blizzard, lounge on the beach all August *sans* sunscreen, and have bareback sex with promiscuous, needle-sharing heroin addicts (or just one, as the case may be).

Really. No matter how dangerous to ourselves or potentially costly to the Medicare and social welfare systems of this country, no one can prevent us from making these decisions. And I believed then, as I do now, that bike helmets belong in the same category: the risk of death or serious brain injury one runs riding without one is low enough that I'm willing to chance it, as I do with so many other (objectively moronic) activities every day.

◆   ◆   ◆

Don't worry … I'm not going to start yowling about the Dangers of the Nanny State here, because I know I'll end up sounding like even more of a Unabomber-ish crank than I actually am. Nor am I going to try and convince you that the relatively minor infringement of liberty represented by mandatory bike helmets put Vancouver on some sort of "slippery slope" to a bleak, neo-Orwellian-future. I'm just saying that, to my mind, the law was logically inconsistent, patronizing, intrusive and unnecessary.

And that's a re-assuring thing. 'Cause Vancouver was really in the minority on this question … most everywhere else in Canada leaves the matter up to the individual adult involved.

In fact, for the most part, this country has managed to do a half-decent job at avoiding the more onerous and intrusive limits on its citizens' personal liberties. And still being free to choose—even (hell, <u>especially</u>) when we opt for the idiotic—is another reason (as if one were needed) to enjoy being Canadian.

Heritage Minute: Yes We Can

Annex area, Toronto, Ontario, November 4, 2008:

They were in Mary's living room, all standing now, wine-glasses raised in honest joy.
"Well, it's official," pronounced a grinning Lloyd Robertson from the television.
"CTV's Decision Desk confirms that <u>Barack Obama</u> *has been elected 44th president of the United States!"*
Mary slipped her arm around Tim's waist and leaned into him.
"Everything's going to be all right ..." she whispered, tears trickling softly down her cheeks.

Un-American Activities

◆

"Are You Now, Or Have You Ever Been, A Hoser?"

I'm about as pro-Canadian as the next guy (assuming the next guy has spent an irretrievable portion of his precious, non-returnable life tapping out a paean to Pogey, Poutine and/or Fur-bearing Aquatic Rodents, and then trying vainly to sell the misbegotten results to an entirely disinterested publishing community).

Still, I'd be the first to admit that there's a lot to like, and even admire, about our Yankee cousins: their relentless pursuit of excellence, for instance, rather than our comfortable bronze-medal complacency; their unabashed celebration of success, rather than our ritual decapitation of "tall poppies;" their brashness, innovation and uncouth energy, rather than our diffidence, deference and maddening risk-aversion.

But "like, and even admire" can only take you so far: as Canadians, the very core of our identity is grounded in low-level hostility towards, defensive prejudice against, and sour-grapes resentment of, the US of A. And it has always been thus, ever since our Loyalist ancestors turned their disdainful backs on the new Republic (not to mention that subsequent "unpleasantness" in 1812).

Plus—and let's be perfectly honest here—a lot of the time, that "drive and enthusiasm" stuff can kinda grate on Canadian nerves. In fact, it can come across as "pushy and overbearing," "loud and obnoxious," or even "ignorant and arrogant" (seriously, you ever listen to any of that "indispensable nation" and "America as a shining city on the hill" drivel?)

◆   ◆   ◆

Don't get me wrong ... we could surely have worse neighbors (I mean "neighbours"). But I'm just as happy not to be a Yank; indeed, Not Being American is, to my mind, a helluva good reason to enjoy Being Canadian.

Test Your Knowledge: Social Values!!!

While Canadians are in many respects quite similar to our American friends, we also tend to have very different attitudes on a whole host of social issues. To help clarify your own feelings towards some of these, please choose the <u>one</u> response that, in your opinion, is most nearly correct:

1. To me, Canada's policy of "Official Bilingualism" constitutes a(n):

    a) low-level annoyance, irritation.
    b) essential recognition of the importance of our Two Founding Nations.
    c) unsuccessful attempt to mollify Quebec nationalists and defang separatism.
    d) just-successful-enough attempt to mollify Quebec nationalists and defang separatism.
    e) big part of the Liberal party's insidious, decades-old, crypto-Commie plot to French-ify the country and destroy our proud British heritage.
    f) useful attempt to balance the national playing field and ensure fairness to an important minority group.
    g) cynical strategy to perpetuate the power of a narrow Central Canadian elite.
    h) inadequate, insulting, completely-missing-the-point attempt to derail the historical inevitability of Quebecois independence.
    i) subtle form of affirmative action for Francophones.
    j) prime reason that our civil service has descended into mediocrity.
    k) not-insignificant cause of Western alienation.
    l) textbook example of the proverbial "tail wagging the dog."
    m) great opportunity to broaden one's horizons, learn another language.
    n) clear sign that Canadians are much more tolerant, compassionate and intelligent than Americans.
    o) expensive and cumbersome attempt at social engineering.
    p) blatantly unfair joke, given Quebec's predilection for unconstitutional sign laws, Bill 101, etc.

2. Canadians also typically have a very different perception of firearms than Americans (for whom gun ownership is arguably enshrined in their constitution). To my personal way of thinking, a gun is:

a) something to be pried from my cold, dead fingers should the powers-that-be ever try to outlaw it.

b) a useful tool to kill troublesome varmints.

c) a useful tool to kill dozens of strangers at a mall or fast-food restaurant on the day that I finally snap.

d) an inanimate object that doesn't kill people (<u>people</u> kill people).

e) an inanimate object that doesn't kill people (<u>dangerous minorities</u> kill people).

f) a symbolic, flagrantly Freudian means of overcompensating for my undersized penis.

g) something on which city and country dwellers will never see eye-to-eye.

3. Similarly, Canada's controversial decade-old "long-gun registry" represents a(n):

a) sinister attempt to identify all potential resistance before black helicopters full of UN troops swoop in to impose the Bilderbergers' dark, Illuminati-inspired commands.

b) insulting waste of time and two billion dollars, given that criminals don't register their smuggled-'cross-the-border Saturday Night Specials, and middle-aged duck hunters are no threat to anyone but themselves.

c) infringement of basic property rights and individual civil liberties guaranteed by English common law.

d) excellent way to get firearms off the street, eliminate violence.

e) pinko-fruity plot by effete elites to destroy traditional rural life.

f) boondoggle which diverts scarce resources from policing, which might be effective, to a bureaucratic "fig leaf," which demonstrably isn't.

g) clear precursor to Armageddon, and eventually Satan's New World Order.

h) disappointment.

4. Canadians also hold different views than Americans on the proper role of their military. For me, the optimum use of this country's armed forces would involve:

a) peacekeeping.

b) wiping out the Taliban.

c) expelling the Acadians to Louisiana (again).

d) enacting the "War Measures Act" in Quebec (can never tell when there'll be another "apprehended insurrection").

e) searching for "Weapons of Mass Destruction" in the Middle East.

f) imposing corrupt, kleptocratic dictatorships on banana republics.

g) assisting in the "soft diplomacy" appropriate to a "middle power."

h) enforcing the Kyoto Accord in Alberta.

i) restoring democracy to Cuba.

j) restoring democracy to Akwesasne.

k) coming to the aid of Canadians in the event of natural disasters.

l) retaking the islands of St. Pierre and Miquelon from France.

m) safeguarding our sovereignty over the Arctic (back off, Denmark … we might actually be able to beat you!)

n) a sudden *coup d'etat.*

Answers:

1) k 2) g 3) h 4) k.

Multiculturalism

◆

"Diversity Makes Us Stronger! ... What Do You Mean, How? ... It Just <u>Does</u>, Okay!"

So I was in the "Eight Items or Less" aisle at Loblaws the other week, idly people-watching to pass the time, when it occurred to me that I was the only white person in line; in fact, since the other six or seven customers, as well as the cashier, were non-Caucasian, I was, technically and temporarily, a "visible minority."

Not that that this disturbed me at all (heaven forfend ... I'd be up in front of a human rights commission faster than you can say "Mark Steyn is a dangerous thought criminal"). Nope, far from it—as immigrants are, for the most part, the only people who seem to truly appreciate this country, I'm inclined to like them way <u>more</u> than I do a lot of their eternally aggrieved and incessantly bickering co-Canadians of longer tenure (was gonna take my routine swipe at Quebecers here, but, really, the rest of us are almost as bad).

And I believe the Charter of Rights obliges me to burble breathlessly on for a paragraph or two now about how deeply I value the rich cornucopia of tasty ethnic foods and smiley-faced Canada Day folk-dancing troupes that have so enriched our formerly Miracle-Whip-on-Yorkshire-Pudding-and-overcooked-vegetables society.

That said, you gotta wonder once in a while if importing 250,000 Highly Diverse people a year into our biggest cities, year after year after year, is an entirely sound long-term strategy. Granted, all indications are that this virtually unprecedented foray into demographic transformation is—entirely against the odds—turning out better than we had any right to expect.

But I'm probably not the only citizen who worries a little that something important might be getting lost, or at least diluted, somewhere. Is "being Canadian" the same for me as it is for the shopkeeper from Shanghai and the nurse from Beirut; the student from Delhi and the grandma from Manila; the agnostic engineer from Cairo and the born-again bricklayer from Palermo; the single-mom bureaucrat from Montego Bay and the gay dentist from Brasilia?

Where is the common bond of understanding between, say, a Second World War veteran in Moncton and a Burmese refugee in Regina; a Sikh mechanic in Abbotsford and a Cree punk-rock drummer in Winnipeg; a Tamil gang-banger in Mississauga and a *pure laine* car salesman in Riviere du Loup; a Somali college professor in St. John's and a Ukrainian construction worker in Hamilton? Will we continue to share enough with each other to be a real nation, or is Canada in danger of becoming Yann Martel's "greatest hotel on Earth?"

Damned if I know ... still, one way or another, we're gonna see how this grand experiment plays out over time. And, odds are, whatever the result, we'll still enjoy being Canadian.

Heritage Minute: The Unhealthy Barber

Edmonton, Alberta, January 8, 2001:

Janine and Richard sat side by side, examining the TD Waterhouse Web-Broker Account information displayed on their computer screen.
"Well, that's it," *said Janine.* "Looks like it's activated and ready to go."
"Yup," *said Richard.*
"Now it's just a matter of transferring funds from our home equity line of credit and buying the shares."
"Jesus, I don't know, honey," *said Richard hesitantly.* "I still have some qualms about borrowing against the condo for this … ."
Janine sighed with exasperation: "Look, we've been through it a thousand times … this is classic leveraging, and the interest'll be tax-deductible … ."
"But <u>Nortel</u> stock …."
"I know it looks scary right now - but remember what Amanda Lang said on Squeeze Play - the best time to buy is when there's blood in the streets."
"Yeah, and that O'Leary guy warned about any blood in the streets being from catching a falling knife … said his "whacking stick" was out for Nortel … ."
"Well, still, it's basic risk/reward, Richard … the stock was, like, $120 six months ago, and closed below $33 today … how much further could it go down? Anyway, even if it does drop more, we've got a good time-horizon … it's at least 2010 before either of us retires and we <u>need</u> the money … . "
"I guess you're right… even if the shares go back up to half of what they were last year, we'll basically double our money … all right, let's do it!"

RRSPs

✦

"Freedom 75"

This country's banks, insurance companies and mutual-fund firms (being the public-spirited corporate citizens that they are) sponsor an annual information campaign, peaking each January/February, that very helpfully reminds us all of the pressing need to save for retirement. (Or, more accurately, they run a shit-load of scary commercials every winter, warning us that we face an old age of dog-food-on-day-old-bread-sandwiches-in-a-dingy-thin-walled-inner-city-rooming-house if we don't start investing with them from the very week that we are conceived.)

Of course, given all the other demands on your typical Canadian's finite resources—student loan, car payments, mortgage, insurance, womb-to-master's-degree subsidization of ungrateful snot-nosed offspring, extortionate income/sales/liquor and property taxes, NHL tickets—it's not so easy to find a few extra nuts to squirrel away for the future. (Hell, you're lucky to have enough left to buy this idiotic book!)

That's why our government, in yet another example of its own near-boundless benevolence (or possibly 'cause it fears having to support us itself), permits we average working schmucks a single, precious, tax-sheltered means of providing for our Golden Years: the Registered Retirement Savings Plan (RRSP).

This scheme, as you doubtless already know, lets Canadians hive off up to 18 percent of each year's earnings into a tax-free investment account, thereby allowing for a nice little refund upfront, and—through the magic of compounding returns over the intervening decades—eventual automatic millionaire-hood.

(Indeed—judging by the aforementioned mutual-fund propaganda—you also automatically acquire a full, leonine head of distinguished-looking gray hair, along with a powerful watercraft; adoring, well-behaved grandkids; fawning, desperately-want-to-assure-their-place-in-the-will adult children;

and a svelte, silver-fox spouse with whom to stroll hand-in-hand along white-sand tropical beaches.)

•   •   •

Some heretics will tell you that RRSPs are a mixed blessing, at best—that, with your luck, you'll work and slave most of your life, deny yourself and defer consumption, only to drop dead from a massive coronary the day before you're scheduled to pick up the gold watch.

Or, if you dodge the Reaper long enough to actually reach retirement, you'll find that everything taken out of an RRSP is taxed at your highest-possible marginal rate, and renders you too "well-off" to benefit from various government benefits/services for which you would otherwise have been eligible (as is the compassionate Canadian way, those goodies are reserved to assist some feckless "grasshopper" who never spared a second's thought for the future).

And, when you come right down to it, these critics have a point. Still, why would you expect the powers-that-be to stop playing ya for a sucker at this stage of the game? It ain't fair, exactly—still, you can take some pride in being one of the self-reliant, prudent, Atlas-like stooges upon whose shoulders the whole ramshackle edifice has always rested.

The kind of person that helps everyone else enjoy being Canadian.

Test Your Knowledge: Personal Finance!!!

Investing effectively for retirement is one of the most important, and complex, responsibilities we face in our everyday lives. To gauge your overall financial knowledge, please choose the one best response to each of these questions:

1. For my personal RRSP account, I tend to:

    a) go into a blind panic on the afternoon of February 28, then race to the bank and throw whatever I have in the chequing account into my plan.

    b) take a cash advance on my Mastercard to contribute, intending to pay it off with the tax refund, then squander said refund on big-screen TVs, high-end restaurant meals and/or a nice trip.

    c) diversify my savings into all of the main asset classes (bonds, equities, cash, REITs, perhaps a small position in precious metals).

d) dollar-cost average into a balanced mutual fund throughout the year.

e) throw the "I Ching" to help me choose an "ethical fund."

2. A sound strategy for my non-registered investments would be to:

a) buy real estate (they're not makin' any more).

b) buy Beanie Babies (they're not makin' any more).

c) concentrate on bank and other high-yielding blue chip stocks that have a long history of raising dividends.

d) focus on energy stocks, with a view to profiting from eventual "Peak Oil."

e) focus on the up-and-coming BRIC countries (Brazil, Russia, India, China).

f) "buy and hold."

g) search for overlooked "value" stocks.

h) pile into the best "growth" stocks.

i) purchase Canada Savings Bonds through a salary-deduction program at work.

j) get gold fillings.

k) take any extra money I have on hand and flush it down the toilet (same results, only faster).

3. My best investment outcome to date involved:

a) wine futures.

b) commemorative coins from the Franklin Mint.

c) a Mexican timeshare.

d) Amway.

e) Bernie Madoff.

f) a chain letter.

g) day-trading tech stocks.

h) scalping "Blue Jays" tickets.

i) hydroponic equipment, marijuana seeds.

j) flipping condos.

k) an emu ranch.

l) my own 1-900 number.

m) a VLT and bucket of quarters.

n) a sockful of batteries and watchful loitering near an ATM.

o) a calculated risk.

4. In contrast, my worst investing experience involved:

a) Nortel, of course.
b) Bre-X.
c) Enron.
d) Barings Bank.
e) Lehman Brothers.
f) Worldcom.
g) Pets.com.
h) Canadian Airlines.
i) any other airline in the world.
j) the Japanese Nikkei.
k) income trusts and Jim Friggin' Flaherty.
l) a hedge fund.
m) a labour-sponsored fund.
n) the Big Three automakers.
o) helping out that Nigerian prince.
p) a good deal of regretful hindsight.

Answers:

1) d 2) c 3) o 4) p.

Westjet

✦

"Because Owners Care"

You know, it's reached the point that I would honestly prefer having a tooth filled at the dentist to flying anywhere on Air Canada.

It's a shame, too, 'cause this country-boy actually used to look forward to plane travel—when I was a young fella, it felt like the very height of jet-setting excitement: soaring effortlessly above the clouds to some exotic locale (like Moncton or maybe even Regina!), sipping an endless series of free drinks-on-demand, waited on hand and foot by cheerful, long-legged stewardesses with a come-hither-and-do-me look... .

...Well, all right, I guess I never did run into too many of those nubile Air Canada angels with boudoir eyes (even back in the day, before they all dried up into prune-faced "flight attendants"). But the sense of adventure (and the free booze) were real enough.

It's a starkly different story these days, though—near as I can tell, whatever frayed and fading romanticism was left of the whole flying experience perished about 15, 20 years ago.

Now, we have to drag ourselves outta bed at 3 a.m. so as to arrive at the airport the requisite 14 hours prior to boarding; then mill around with the rest of the dazed herd for an hour or so looking for an open check-in counter; wait in a lineup so long that it eventually develops its own regional sub-dialect; get to the head of the queue, only to do verbal battle with some twitchy-eyed gorgon in the early stages of her latest nervous breakdown (and sporting an actual, honest-to-goodness <u>chip</u> on her shoulder ... salt 'n vinegar, it smells like); and finally check your bag/pay the excess weight fee (on top of the additional fuel and security surcharges, airport improvement fees, GST, PST, etc., that have already added about 50 percent to your advertised fare...).

After which it's time to proceed through the patent absurdities and small humiliations of security screening ... carry-on opened and underwear rifled through; Pepsi, hair gel and nail clippers confiscated, crotch intimately "wanded" by some minimum-wage rent-a-flunky (who, judging by the accent, was recruited that very morning as he stepped off his own Third World Airways flight onto Canadian soil for the first time and waited in his own line to file a refugee claim).

At last, mercifully, you're through, and free to spend the remaining six hours in departure-lounge purgatory, rooting through the recycling bin for discarded newspapers and resignedly checking your watch every four minutes. Then boarding: you shuffle along the aisle at the speed of mammalian evolution; reach your cramped last-row seat; clamber over the obligatory fat businessman with visible sweat stains the size of dinner plates under each arm; and awkwardly wedge yourself in beside the frazzled teen-mother clutching her feverish, squirming, colicky infant.

Following which it's just a matter of X many hours of hemmed-in boredom, broken only by the approach of surly flight-battleaxes bearing two-dollar mini-cans of Pringles and six-dollar Molsons (consumption of which compels you to crawl over the obese and by now seemingly comatose business-slob and wait ten minutes in fidgety, discreetly cross-legged discomfort before entering the reeking, pitching, photo-booth-sized washroom, for which the British euphemism "Water Closet" would really seem more appropriate).

Then, finally, finally, finally, you land; endure the interminable interval before deplaning; grunt a grudging response to the air crew's painfully insincere "buh-byes;" and sharp-elbow your way into the suppressed hysteria of the luggage-carousel mob (knowing full well that you could be napping on a bench, 'cause your bag—if it arrived in this city at all—is gonna be third-last down the chute, same as always). And at last you droop out of the terminal, already frozen with dread at the prospect of the nightmarish return trip.

(All of this is under ideal conditions, of course; should there be a storm, or a computer-system glitch, or, indeed, an unexpected event of any kind—like, for example, "Winter"—then you get to spend three nights in a row sleeping on the Halifax airport floor; or New Year's Eve snuggled up to a payphone, grooving to the latest Bollywood Muzak as you wait for customer-support in Bangalore to rebook you; or Christmas Day huddled morosely in the corner of a Pearson bar, nursing a ten-dollar draft... .)

◆   ◆   ◆

Air Canada, then, combines the very worst features of a hidebound, sclerotic bureaucracy with those of a price-gouging, bloodsucking, for-profit corporation. And it'd be ten times more vile in the absence of some viable competition ... which is why all Canadians—whether or not they ever have occasion to patronize the firm—should enjoy having Westjet around.

Heritage Minute: *Deux Solitudes*

Beach bar, Phuket, Thailand, January 2008:

"Crikey, where you been, mate?" asked the taller Aussie.
"Saw a Canadian flag on that fella's fanny pack and figured I'd say 'Hi,'" said the Haligonian. "Guy was from Quebec City, though, so we couldn't really understand each other…"
"All you polar-bear fuckers learn Frog Lingo in school, dontcha?"
"Kinda. But if ya don't use it, ya forget it. Hell, I can communicate easier with you kangaroo-diddlers than with most French-Canadians…"
"Oi, a dingo's ate me baby!" interjected the blond Aussie, in a mocking falsetto. "Whose round is it, anyways?"

Miscellaneous

✦

"A Few More Reasons to Enjoy Being Canadian That, While Undeniably True, Cannot Really Be Padded Out Into Individual Chapters"

Cirque du Soleil --- dude, that shit is incredible!

Feel of sunshine on your bare arms in April, on that precious first day of the year when it's warm enough to slip your jacket off for a few minutes.

Smell of distant early-evening barbecue on the Victoria Day long weekend.

Maple Leaf Flag --- I know, I know, it was invented by Lester Pearson's brain trust in the '60's as a form of subliminal advertising for the Liberal party colours. Still, you've gotta admit, it's gone on to be a textbook example of successful branding, instantly recognizable and, for the most part, positively regarded around the world (at least according to American backpackers in Europe).

And, having grown up with it, I'd have to say that I'm pretty fond of the old girl.

Net-filing your Income Tax Return --- makes it a helluva lot easier to cheat, eh? (Although heaven help us if CRA ever comes back and asks for receipts!)

Charities --- we've got a lot of groups in this country that do great, necessary work for people, and I'm glad to donate a few bucks to some of them. Of course—being, as I may have mentioned elsewhere, a really, really, really cheap prick—I'm even gladder to get a tax credit to partially offset whatever I've given.

And this little plum is, by government standards, not ungenerous: the first $200.00 you donate is eligible for a federal tax credit of 15 percent (plus corresponding provincial credits), which increases to 29 percent (plus provincial yada-yada) on higher amounts. Even better, you're allowed to combine receipts with your spouse, and carry unclaimed donations forward for up to five years, thereby maximizing the family's eventual refund.

Aside from this obvious boon, though, I've noticed one that is slightly more subtle: most of the charities I support try to pull in <u>further</u> donations by mailing me various pieces of useful merchandise (key-tags, greeting cards, personalized notepads, home address labels, etc.)

Respond to this come-on once, as I did a few years back, and the group (not unreasonably) then redoubles its efforts by sending even more of the item that apparently jogged your generosity. All the time. Month after year after decade, whether or not you ever again contribute.

And, if you're even luckier, they'll sell your mailing details down the river and get you placed on a charity "sucker list"—now, I've got diseases I've never heard of sending me boxes of helpful goodies on a regular basis, to the point where I haven't had to buy a Christmas or birthday card in years. Heck of a deal, no?

<u>Highway of Heroes</u> --- you've probably seen this little procession dozens of times by now on the news ... a motorcade bearing the remains of one (or more) of our Afghanistan casualties from a military airbase in Trenton, Ontario, to the coroner's office in Toronto. And every single time one rolls through, hundreds of ordinary citizens turn out on the overpasses—as near as I can tell spontaneously—to wave the flag and pay their respects.

Which I can't help but feel is a real touch of class ...

<u>Imperial System</u> --- quick, how tall are you? Uh-huh, and how much do you weigh? Okay, now what's that in centimeters and kilos?

Dunno, do ya? Thirty-five years after Trudeau wrenched us kicking and screaming into a brave new world of weights and measures, and we still can't use metric with any consistency. (Or won't ... I'm so stubborn that I continue to describe my parents' place in Nova Scotia as being "six miles outside of Louisbourg.")

Granted, we've all pretty much bought into "kilometers per hour" and "degrees Celsius." But we still order 16-ounce slabs o' steak at the "Keg," and throw ten-pound turkeys into the oven for Thanksgiving (20 minutes a pound at 325 degrees Fahrenheit). And we flop down on our sofas to watch CFL football (which continues to be played on a field measured in yards) on 32-inch TVs in our soon-to-be-foreclosed-upon 1,500-square-foot homes ....

... So, basically, Canadians persist in exhibiting the kind of retrograde, illiberal, deeply unprogressive behaviour that must have poor Pierre E.

Trudeau a-spinnin' in his grave (not least 'cause he's always be six <u>feet</u> under in our hearts).

And, while we're at it, here are a handful of things that, with the best of wills, I cannot bring myself to enjoy about our home and native land:

<u>Beer</u> --- it pains me to admit this, it really does, but here goes: most Canadian beer (by which I mean the mega-brewed pot-bellied-pig-swill churned out by our now-almost-entirely-foreign-owned-but-that's-no-excuse suds oligopoly) is actually not very good.

I'm serious. Ever taste a Molson's "Export?" A Keith's "India Pale Ale?" A Labatt's "Blue," fer chrissake? Oh, sure, they'd all still clean the clock of any American brand you put in the ring against 'em (if only for that precious additional percent-and-a-half of alcohol). But that's not really a fair fight, is it—American brew is truly awful, a concoction so vile that it scarcely merits inclusion in the "refreshing beverage" category. No, what we should be doing is comparing our beer with that quaffed in the rest of the world.

And if you do, my friend, you'll be forced to acknowledge the bitter truth … ours is middling, at best. (Sorta the same as the sacred Canadian health-care system—yeah, okay, it easily outclasses the mucked-up Yankee model, but try measuring our version against those found anywhere else in the developed world and we're <u>well</u> back of the pack.)

<u>Crybaby advocacy groups that get public funding to sue the government and force it to spend a bunch of tax dollars on some alleged social ill</u> --- if the sumbitches feel that strongly about it, let 'em raise their own money to launch a legal challenge, or enlist some fellow-traveling lawyer to take the case on *pro freakin' bono,* like they did back in the '60s. Quit putting <u>my</u> money where your (perpetually indignant and constantly flapping) mouth is.

<u>Quebec separatists</u> --- used to enrage me, but now they're just a bore … get over yourselves, assholes.

<u>Municipal public-service unions subjecting regular people (i.e., the freakin' PUBLIC) to substantial hardship in order to preserve some feature of an already over-generous labour contract, like bankable sick days that can be "cashed out" upon retirement</u> --- hey, we're all lookin' out for Number One. But if you want to, for example, deprive old/sick/poor people of their bus system for two months during the depths of an Ottawa winter, or bury Toronto in mounds of putrefying garbage for half the summer, then you've crossed the friggin' line, jerks!

<u>Daylight Savings Time</u> --- never thought much about this one until I moved back from Japan, which somehow built itself up from a bomb-blasted post-war moonscape to the globe's second-biggest economy without ever adopting the Western world's peculiar fetish for semi-annual clock-changes.

But really, when you look at it, are the (very minor, and largely amorphous) benefits that allegedly accrue from this burdensome exercise really worth the twice-yearly hassle?

Kudos to Saskatchewan for steadfastly resisting this unnecessary foolishness … would that the rest of us were as sensible.

<u>Nunavut</u> --- Canada subsidizes this make-believe jurisdiction to the tune of $40,000 per inhabitant per year. Could its 30,000 residents not have stayed part of the Northwest Territories and saved us some portion of that sum?

<u>Canada Geese</u> --- notoriously vile-tempered; prodigious and indiscriminate defecators (usually in parks and other public places where you might want to play Frisbee or flop down on the grass for a snooze); and distressingly prone to diving headlong into the jet engines of passenger-bearing airplanes. Why do we allow this foul creature to sully our nation's good name?

<u>Guv'nors</u> --- if you stop and think about it (and I'm willing to bet that your mind bends to the subject with merciful infrequency), the Governor General of Canada is an expensive and faintly ridiculous anachronism … a sort of Gilded, Medieval-style Parasite, if you will.

As many of us were surprised to discover in December 2008, however, the GG <u>does</u> still have an important constitutional role to play from time to time (that is, whenever the sinister forces of separatism, socialism and pitiful self-delusion coalesce into a mortal threat to Harperite rule).

Plus, our recent-year strategy of staffing the job entirely with female CBC journalists o' colour can probably be counted as a public-relations plus in the wider world, thereby giving Canada the type of multi-culti street cred that so many of us seem to crave.

Still, while I'm willing to cut the Governor General a bit of slack, I defy anyone to justify the existence of this nation's ten provincial <u>lieutenant governors</u> … useless sods, the lot of 'em!

Conclusion

So there you have it—your basic tale told by an idiot, full of sound and fury (and warm, furry beavers), signifying nothin'.

'Cause, despite the section-title up above, there is no real "conclusion" to be drawn from any of this—I have no profound, hard-won insights into the national psyche to share; there will be no trembly-lipped tributes to (or foam-flecked diatribes against) "tolerance," "compromise" and all-holy "diversity" here; still less do I intend to engage in any John-Ralston-Saul-style gibbering about our "Métis Soul."

No, the only thing I've got for you that even resembles a "point" is the same modest one we started out with in the Introduction: that, metaphorically speaking, Canada's glass is <u>at least</u> three-quarters full; that "being Canadian" is, on the whole, a positive and enjoyable gig; that, if you compare the extraordinary freedom, opportunity and abundance in which we live with the conditions faced by our own ancestors (or, indeed, by billions of our contemporaries elsewhere in the world <u>right now</u>), Canadians have it pretty friggin' good indeed.

And it would be nice (albeit entirely uncharacteristic) if we could put the non-stop coast-to-coast-to-coast bitching on pause every once in a while and count our goddamn blessings. Eh!!!

Alternate Realities (1): 2006

A furtive figure stole along the corridor of the House of Commons, head swiveling suspiciously as it checked for any sign of pursuit.

Finding none, it slunk into a nearby conference room and hastily locked the door, turning at last to survey the small group of sinister, monk-cowled beings within. "Hail, Brothers," the figure said, after a long moment.

"Hail, ex-prime minister Paul Martin," the group intoned. "Hail Victory." One by one the members removed their hoods, revealing the baleful visages of Stephen Harper, Ralph Klein, Mike Harris, Stockwell Day and David Frum. Each of their robes was emblazoned with a curious logo: *Vast Right-Wing Conspiracy (Canada Chapter)*.

Harper stepped forward first and grasped Martin's right hand in both of his. "You poor man, you've been through so much!" he said with great feeling.

"Yes," admitted Martin, "but it's well worth it to help weaken the Liberal party and advance our heartless conservative cause!" At this, the others roared their approval and began pressing expensive cigars and flutes of champagne upon the newcomer.

"Really, you were masterful," praised a purse-lipped David Frum. "There's no way this dead-eyed automaton," he nodded sourly toward Harper "would be prime minister today without your surrealistically awful performance in the job."

"Well, it was very, very important to Canadians!" deadpanned Martin, inspiring renewed torrents of merriment all around.

"Ha, ha, yes!" laughed Stockwell Day, rollerblading over to slap Martin's buttocks (twice, guiltily). "You've created such a level of disgust with government that working people nation-wide will endorse—nay, demand—tax cuts that disproportionately benefit the amoral corporations and rich Americans we serve...."

... At the mention of "Americans," the assembled plotters at once began frisking about the room, goose-stepping in delight and chanting "profits before people, profits before people!"

"Privatize 'em all and let God sort 'em out," slurred Klein at last, before guzzling noisily from one of the champagne bottles he was clutching and keeling over.

... "And then the way will be clear to implement our hidden social agenda of intolerance, homophobia, bigotry, and the like," Day finished darkly, a far-off look in his eyes.

The others stirred uneasily and cast shifty looks about the room. "Ssshh! That's to remain a secret until the time is right! ... Er, anyway, Brother Paul," said Harper, quickly changing the subject, "you are to be congratulated. There's been no "mole" of your caliber discrediting our ideological enemies among voters since...."

Suddenly there came a low knock at the door. All froze except Day, who skated forward, necktie knotted Rambo-like around his head, and unlocked it. He backed warily away in a martial arts combat crouch as an ominous, ratlike figure stealthily entered.

"Ah, there he is at last," Harper burst out in relief. "We were just talking about you."

"Hail, Brothers," it said.

"Hail, former Ontario premier Bob Rae," they intoned.

Top ten over-the-top Canadian similes

As forlorn as the *Maple Leafs'* playoff hopes
As satisfying as seeing Conrad Black in prison
As irrelevant as the Genie Awards
As dim-witted as letting CTV buy the *Hockey Night in Canada* theme song
As disappointed as a Plains of Abraham battle re-enactor
As awkward as New Democrats dancing
As scarce as streets named after Lucien Bouchard in Red Deer
As tasteless as an Air Canada sandwich
As dead as the Avro Arrow
As hopeless as trying to drive through a *Surete du Quebec* speed trap with Ontario plates

Top ten over-the-top (and really "dry") Canadian similes

As cheerful as the Greyhound bus terminal in Saskatoon
As popular as a be-turbanned Sikh Mountie at the Legion
As serene as last call in Cape Breton
As comfortable as Stephen Harper kissing a baby
As well-deserved as a Canada Council grant
As likely as a moment of silence for Mordecai Richler at the Quebec National Assembly
As clear and unambiguous as a referendum question on sovereignty-association
As successful as Ernie Eves
As believable as a pledge to scrap the GST, fix Medicare for all time, and/or eradicate child poverty by the year 2000
As welcome as Ezra Levant carrying a six-pack of wine coolers and a copy of *The Satanic Verses* into your local mosque

Top ten over-the-top similes for everyday life

As unsettling as a grey pubic hair
As perfunctory as a Tuesday afternoon stripper
As dismal as visiting your brother-in-law in prison
As smug as a white Yuppie couple showing off their newly adopted Chinese baby
As disturbing as catching an "on-the-street" news crew filming you from the neck down for the third time this year
As scarce as black people at an *AC/DC* concert

As platitudinous as the Dalai Lama
As eerily in sync as local gasoline prices
As awkward as when your dog watches you have sex
As shallow as celebrity Kabbalah

Top ten "dry" similes for everyday life

As deeply appreciated as an SUV-load of bottled water at a Greenpeace meeting
As happy as a charter flight-load of passengers on their way back from March break in Cancun
As natural as Madonna's British accent
As soothing as *Kraftwerk*
As trustworthy as a time-share pitch given by a crack-whore
As attractive as that razor-cut hairstyle that all too many Chinese guys get
As welcome as an early-morning Jehovah's Witness
As easy to get as a mail-in rebate
As reasonably priced as a beer in Whistler
As classy as a McDonalds in a Walmart

Top ten over-the-top Canadian comparatives

Slower than Stockwell Day trying to master trigonometry
Bigger than Pierre Berton's ego
Deeper than Brian Mulroney's voice during a bout of pneumonia
Longer than an MRI waiting list in Ontario
Scarier than TASER-wielding Mounties at the airport
Sadder than the day Gretzky was traded to LA
A shorter life-expectancy than Clifford Olson in Gen Pop
Stripped faster than a Porsche parked overnight at the corner of Jane and Finch
Gone quicker than Ralph Klein with a fistful of beer tickets
More holes in it than Margaret Trudeau's brain
Less coverage than a Natural Law Party campaign rally
More chemistry than Peter Mackay and Condi Rice

Alternate Realities (2): Dreaming in Technicolo(u)r

"... And dat's how da Global Green Shift can cut carbone emission in 'aff by 2030," concluded Canadian prime minister Stephane Dion, gesturing vaguely over his podium at a large overhead projection.

The assembled world dignitaries gaped at him in stunned silence; only the scraping of a few media pencils broke the disbelieving stillness. Then, suddenly, the tension collapsed on itself and wave after wave of delighted applause rolled across the jam-packed auditorium.

"Brilliant," gushed the UN Secretary-General, pumping Dion's hand wildly as they strode from the stage. "Absolutely brilliant! Explained that way, I don't know how we could have missed the solution before, I really don't!"

"It no t'ing," said Dion, deftly side-stepping the first of an excited throng of well-wishers.

"You'll get another Peace Prize for this, mark my words!" shouted Pope John Paul IV from amidst the swirling crowd. "Bless you, my son!"

"*Merci*, t'ank you, Pope," replied the PM in a modest tone, continuing to work his way slowly through the adulatory mob. At last, the nimble politico was able to break free and bound up a nearby flight of stairs, easily leaving a pack of reporters puffing vainly in his wake, and finally ducking into a secure suite reserved for him at the top.

"*Sacre Bleu, Michel*, not bad, eh?"

"Yes," replied long-time deputy prime minister Michael Ignatieff, forcing a stiff facsimile of a smile and handing his sweaty leader a towel. "Yes, you've triumphed once more. I'm very happy for you."

Dion ignored him, distracted by a copy of the *Globe and Mail* recently couriered in from Toronto. "Unemployment Rate Falls to New Multi-Decade Low" blared the banner headline, atop a smaller sidebar article entitled "US President Jesse Ventura Decries 'Brain Drain' to North."

The grizzled political legend chuckled, relishing the vindication of his long-term vision for a sustainable and vibrant Canadian economy. All the more gratifying, he mused, since the world stage had claimed so much of his attention during this fifth term in office.

As he leafed through the rest of the day's articles, Dion paused occasionally, tsk-tsking wryly at a few of the more bizarre developments. "CTV News Anchor Humiliated by Leaked Video Outtakes" read one; "John Baird Murder Trial Drags On" another; and finally "Federal Opposition Leader Mario Dumont Takes Blame for Latest By-election Rout."

"Life, she is funny, you know," he said contentedly.

Ignatieff, still hovering in the background, agreed with faux-heartiness: "Yes, Prime Minister, that sure is true, sir!"

But Dion wasn't listening; his eyes had been drawn to the paper's op-ed page, where a guest column of compelling elegance and lucidity hailed him as indisputably the greatest environmentalist the world had ever known … the author's name: Al Gore. "Dat incredible," blurted Dion, misty and humbled. "*Merci, mon ami*, you taught me well!" …

●   ●   ●

… "Stephane, Stephane, wake up!" hissed Dion's wife, vigorously shaking him. "Come on, stop dreaming now, eh?"

"Oh, *mon dieu*," said Dion, groggily rubbing the grit from his eyes. "My many triumph must 'ave tired me h'out, ah?"

His wife stared in frank astonishment, and finally sputtered: "Triumphs?" But Dion wasn't listening … his eyes had fallen on the calendar across from him; on it was circled today's date … October 14, 2008 … along with the notation "Election Day" in red ink.

A low groan escaped him as reality flooded in.

Top ten over-the-top obscure comparisons

So macho he makes Mike Holmes look like Paul Lynde

So boring he makes Ken Dryden sound like Robin Williams after a Red Bull and three lines of coke

So flashily dressed he makes Don Cherry look like Kurt Cobain

So bad it made *Porky's Revenge* seem like *Citizen Kane*

So violent it makes *Reservoir Dogs* look like *Fraggle Rock*

So dull it makes a Royal Commission hearing seem like a *Bum Fights* video

So disappointing it makes Paul Henderson's winning goal against the Russians feel like the day after Ben Johnson's steroid test in Seoul

So perky she makes Valerie Pringle look like Ben Stein

So simplistic it makes the "B plot" on *King of Kensington* seem like *The Brothers Karamazov*

So square he makes Preston Manning look like Jeff Spicolli

Top ten over-the-top political comparisons

So right-wing it makes the *National Post* seem like a latter-season *M*A*S*H** script

So left-wing it makes Stephen Lewis preaching about AIDS in Africa sound like Lou Dobbs on a bad chest-hair day

So right-wing he makes Mark Steyn sound like Noam Chomsky

So left-wing it makes *No Logo* read like *Mein Kampf*

So right-wing she makes David Frum sound like a Shining Path guerrilla

So left-wing she makes Maude Barlow sound like Ted Byfield

So right-wing he makes Tom Flanagan sound like Michael Moore

So left-wing she makes Elizabeth May sound like Pat Buchanan

So right-wing he makes Jason Kenney sound like Sting

So left-wing he makes Bruce Cockburn sound like Toby Keith

Top ten over-the-top general comparisons

More credibility-enhancing than a hip black friend

More disappointing than finding *bukkake* porn on your new boyfriend's computer

More pretentious than a 15-year-old who's just discovered Nietzsche

More tangled than an octopuses' orgy

More slippery than a personal-injury lawyer rolled in warm goose shit

More infuriating than George W. Bush's little frat-boy smirk

More relaxing than the smell of newly smoked grass

More unsettling than looking in the kitchen of your favourite Chinese restaurant
More self-indulgent than a film directed by Kevin Costner
More unwelcome than a methadone clinic opening next to your kid's middle school

Top ten over-the-top "cold" comparisons: "Jesus, man, it's colder than ......"

A pawnbroker's heart
The proverbial witch's teat
The south pole of Pluto
Stephen Harper glaring at a CBC reporter
Peter Mansbridge and Wendy Mesley's last on-air interaction before the divorce became final
The end days at Stalingrad
Intercourse in an igloo
New Year's Eve at Portage and Main
The day Jean Chretien handed off his prime ministership to Paul Martin
Walt Disney's cryogenically frozen corpse

Alternate Realities (3):
Public Service Directive

LOS ANGELES – "In a survey of half a dozen recent economic studies conducted in the United States and England, University of Rochester economist Steven Landsburg notes that results all point to a direct correlation between height and income, one at least as dramatic as those involving sex and race ... Researchers have affixed specific salary values to this height-to-earnings ratio: In England, each additional inch in height is associated with a 1.7 percent increase in income. In the United States, each inch is worth 1.8 percent -- the equivalent of about $1,500 a year." (*Globe and Mail*, March 28, 2002)

April 12, 2015, Ottawa – Public Service Commission of Canada

The recent landmark Supreme Court of Canada decision on Height-based Inequality has profound implications for all Canadians, but especially for members of the federal public service.

The ruling in question, to recap, found in favour of the advocacy group Short Humans Ridding Innocent Men of Prejudice and Stereotypes (SHRIMPS) in its class action lawsuit charging pervasive and systemic discrimination against the Vertically Underprivileged.

Evidence heard included these clear and disturbing indications of bias in the work place:

- More than 90 percent of male Fortune 500 executives are of above-average height, and more than half are over six feet tall. In telling contrast, only three percent are under 5'7".
- Men in higher-ranking professional jobs are two inches taller, on average, than those junior to them; this startling discrepancy persists even when age, experience and education are controlled for statistically.

- Male university graduates 6'2" and taller receive starting salaries 12 percent higher than those under six feet.

Such disparities in power and wealth have historically been mirrored in the personal realm. SHRIMPS' case brought into focus the degree to which Vertically Deprived males are stigmatized and disadvantaged in the dominant "Height-centric" culture, and the untold damage to group members' psychological—and even physical—well-being that this has inflicted:

- Only a tiny minority of heterosexual romantic relationships involve a male shorter than a female, thus, through no fault of their own, sharply limiting the pool of potential mates available to men of below-average height.
- Height Underprivileged males are disproportionately bullied, beaten and ridiculed as children and into young adulthood.
- "Short" males are vastly under-represented on sports teams, and those sports in which they do participate are systematically devalued and deprived of financial resources and media attention.
- Deeply-embedded linguistic structures act to injure the self-esteem of our "Short" fellow-citizens (to wit, "it takes a big man to do/say that," "that person lacks stature in the field," "small fry," "runt of the litter," "to come up short," and "to be looked down upon"). Similar forms exist in French, and indeed in all known world languages.

The Supreme Court unanimously agreed that such patent injustice cannot be tolerated in a society striving to be more open, inclusive and sensitive to <u>each</u> of its members. Vertically Challenged Canadians must therefore be treated with the fairness and respect that all historically victimized groups have the right to demand, and it is incumbent upon governments of all levels to take the lead in changing outmoded attitudes and unacceptable conditions.

To facilitate these goals, the Public Service Committee on Height-Discrimination Redress and Reconciliation has recommended that:

- All male federal employees 5'6" or under receive a 12 percent pay equity adjustment to their salaries, effective immediately and retroactive to the adoption of the Canadian Charter of Rights and Freedoms in 1982.
- Future salary levels be monitored for disparities between "Short" employees and other workers.
- Steps be taken to be more welcoming to the Height Deprived—the "glass ceiling" so far above their heads <u>must</u> be shattered by proactive

programs to recruit and promote them to levels commensurate with their share of the labour force.

- Sensitivity training on the subject of Height become mandatory for all employees from April 1, 2016, and active steps be taken to discipline those disparaging or creating a hostile environment for "Short" Canadians in the public service.
- Provincial governments be encouraged to amend human rights legislation to include the "Short."
- Educational systems be improved to provide positive examples of "Short" males, and to institute "zero tolerance" for verbal and physical violence against the Vertically Impoverished.
- A television and poster advertising campaign modeled on those promoting racial and gender sensitivity be mounted to change regressive attitudes toward Height Underprivileged Canadians.

Much more clearly needs to be done, but these preliminary measures go some distance toward creating the kind of Canada we all deserve.